FIRES BURNING

JULIE LAWSON

Stoddart

A GEMINI YOUNG ADULT

First published in 1995 by
Stoddart Publishing Co. Limited
34 Lesmill Road
Toronto, Canada
M3B 2T6
(416) 445-3333

Canadian Cataloguing in Publication Data

Lawson, Julie, 1947-
Fires burning
"Gemini young adult."
ISBN: 0-7736-7430-6
I. Title.

PS8573.A94F5   1995   jC8L3'.54   C94-932790-5
        P27.L38Fi   1995

Cover design: Brant Cowie/ArtPlus
Cover illustration: Laurie McGaw
Typesetting: Tannice Goddard/S.O. Networking
Printed and bound in Canada

*Stoddart Publishing gratefully acknowledges the support of the
Canada Council, the Ontario Ministry of Culture, Tourism, and
Recreation, Ontario Arts Council, and Ontario Publishing
Centre in the development of writing and publishing in Canada.*

To Kathryn Cole –
one thousand
paper cranes
for helping
this story unfold.

Acknowledgements

The author is grateful to Margaret Dyment and her *Write Away!* group for their criticism and support during the early stages of this book. Thanks also to Dawn Schell, Child and Family Counsellor at the Victoria Child Sexual Abuse Society, Dr. C. E. Malinowski, and Judy Robbins, Counsellor, School District #62 (Sooke). And special thanks to Patrick Lawson for his insightful comments.

PART 1

CHELSEA

Chapter 1

"That's it, Chelsea. That's the last straw." Chelsea's mother stormed into the living room, clutching a letter in her hand. "Do you hear me? I've had it!"

Chelsea folded her feelings, one on top of another until she felt as small and tight as a piece of folded paper. She slumped deeper into the sofa, hiding behind her long black hair, and calmly turned the page of her book. Mom could rant and rave all she liked. The last straw kept happening over and over again, one crisis after another. Nothing changed. Same paper, different folds.

Like origami.

She was nine the first time she'd heard the word, seven years ago. "Origami," she had chanted. *Origami*, a magical sound, the word casting a spell.

She ran her fingers over the paper, loving the feel of its glossy surface. A perfect square, one side white, the other coloured. Turquoise, magenta, flaming orange, spring green, colours to brighten the grey November day. Chelsea was lucky; she got red.

Poppy red, perfect for Remembrance Day. Which was why they'd been given origami paper in the first place. To make cranes, a symbol of peace.

"The Japanese believed that cranes live for a thousand years," her teacher had said. "According to a Japanese legend, if you fold a thousand paper cranes, the gods will make your wishes come true. Like Sadako."

Chelsea listened as Mr. Chan told them the story. How two-year-old Sadako had survived the 1945 bombing of Hiroshima, only to get leukemia, the radiation sickness, ten years later. How she had folded cranes in her hospital bed, wishing for a long life, wishing for peace in the world. At the time of her death, she had made 644. "Her friends folded the rest of the cranes," Mr. Chan continued, "because they wanted to honour her memory and share in her wish for peace. Now children all over the world fold origami cranes as a symbol of peace."

"And long life, too?" Chelsea asked.

Her teacher nodded.

"Do you have to be Japanese to believe that?"

Her classmates laughed, the way they always laughed at her questions. Chelsea didn't care. It was important to get things right.

"I don't think so," said Mr. Chan.

"Good." She didn't know anyone who was sick or dying, but you never could tell. Besides, if she made one thousand cranes, the gods might grant her wish — that what happened two weeks ago would not happen again. And with one thousand cranes she might be assured of a long and happy life. If she learned to make them properly.

"Such clever hands," Dad always said, "just like your mother." Like her mother, Chelsea loved to draw and paint, but she preferred paper, sand, clay — anything that could be shaped and transformed into something else. Even cookie dough and mashed potatoes, until Mom put a stop to that. But the cranes looked complicated. And the paper was so beautiful, she couldn't bear the thought of wrecking it.

She listened carefully, following the instructions to the letter. White side up, side to side. Coloured side up, corner to corner . . . Fold down the head and pull out the wings.

"Perfect, Chelsea," said Mr. Chan. "Take some more paper. Make as many as you like. Make a whole flock."

She folded one crane after another until it was time to go home. "I'm going to make hundreds of cranes," she said excitedly, "and hang them from a branch in my room. Do you want to help, Jess? I've got more paper. How about you, Mel? Can you come over?"

No one could come over; no one wanted to help. So what's new? she thought. I'll do it myself. She gathered up her belongings and hurried out of the classroom.

As she walked home, she pictured her room ablaze with origami. Dad was right, she did have clever hands. He had clever eyes. That's why he was such a good photographer. She flew up the stairs and through the door, eager to show him the brightly coloured cranes. Then she stopped.

The hallway felt different. And the living room. Everything looked the same, but something was wrong. Heart pounding, she rushed to her father's darkroom.

The door had been left ajar. That, in itself, was unusual. "Dad?" Cautiously, she pushed open the door.

The room was empty. Cleaned out. Everything gone. Prints, negatives, trays, containers of chemicals, the enlarger . . . "Dad!" she called, frantic. "Dad!"

She heard footsteps on the stairs and ran out, hoping it was him, hoping he'd give a good reason for clearing out his private room. But it was Mom. "Here," she said, handing Chelsea a sheet of paper. "He left you a note."

Chelsea couldn't keep from shaking. Her eyes

darted over the words, flitting from one to another, while her mind tried to decipher the meaning. "For years not getting along." What was this? "Leave Mom to go his own way." What did he mean? "Love you always." What did it matter? He was gone.

A terrible thought struck her. Was it her fault? "You're a dreadful girl to tell lies like that," Mom had shouted two weeks ago. "What would Daddy say? He thinks the world of you, and now this. It's just one story after another with you. How *could* you!"

She thought she heard her mother, now speaking in a gentle voice, trying to explain, but her spoken words were as hard to understand as her father's written ones. Only one thing seemed clear. It *was* her fault. It had to be. Why else would he have gone? Nothing else made sense.

Slowly, she unclenched her fist. What was once a crane with outstretched wings was now a damp, crumpled wad of paper. A smear of red dye trickled across her hand.

"Did you hear me?" Mom's voice, hard as ice, shrieked into her thoughts.

Calmly, Chelsea turned another page.

"You look at me when I'm talking to you!"

Chelsea looked up, her face a mask of indifference.

"See this?" Mom waved the letter in her face.

"It's from your principal. A fire in the washroom! Did you honestly think you wouldn't get caught? You could've burned down the school!"

"But I didn't."

"And now you've got a suspension."

"So? It's June. I've passed my exams. School's almost over."

"A suspension! That's it. I've had it."

"So ground me."

With one sudden movement Mom knocked the book out of Chelsea's hands, grabbed her shirt by the collar, and yanked her off the sofa. "Oh no. Not this time. Nothing so easy as getting grounded. Three days here, five days there, what difference does it make? This time, you're gone. You're out of here."

Something in her mother's voice, something she hadn't heard before, took Chelsea by surprise. Don't get unfolded, she told herself, pressing down the small edge of panic. Stay calm. "Oh? Have you found a foster home for me? I hope it's in a better neighbourhood," she added sarcastically, knowing that few places were better than the West Vancouver neighbourhood she lived in. "Hey, maybe there's even a mother. Might be a nice change from living with a — "

The slap across her face knocked her backwards. "You — !"

"It's true." Chelsea forced her voice to remain calm and steady. "And Simon, that scum you call a boyfriend — " She gasped as her mother hit her again. "Send me anywhere, I don't care."

Her mother struck her on the side of the head, a blow that made her ears ring. "Then it's about time you *did* care! Do you hear me?" She grabbed Chelsea by the shoulders and gave her a violent shake. "You're going to care. One of these days you'll care very much."

Chelsea felt the fingernails digging into her neck and shoulders. She wanted to scream, to stop the shaking, but she wouldn't allow herself to cry out. And she wouldn't lose control by fighting back. Not now. Not this way.

Finally her mother stopped. She stood with her head down, breathing hard, arms hanging loosely at her sides. "Oh God, Chelsea, I'm sorry. If you could just — I didn't mean — "

"What?" Chelsea gave her an icy stare. "You say you're sorry and everything's changed? You say that every time. Nothing ever changes." She brushed past her mother and headed for the stairs, pausing to pick up the letter. "I'm not sorry. So what if I got caught?" She tossed the letter onto the coffee table. "I'd do the same thing again, in a minute. Only ten times worse." She turned and walked upstairs, careful not to let on that the neat packet of feelings was now crumpled and ready to ignite.

Igniting was her specialty. It started after Dad moved away. It started with one match.

Quickly, decisively, she had struck it on the box. Wrinkled her nose at the pungent smell of sulphur, smiled at the explosion of light. She held the match steady, close to her face. Watched the blue-violet flame flare to bright gold and burn its way down. Heard the sudden intake of breath as the flame licked her finger. Then the sizzle as she dropped the match into the glass of water.

She struck another and another, forcing herself to hold on until she could just feel the burn, then letting go.

Later, she moved outside without the precaution of water. She crouched behind the hedge, swept up a pile of dried leaves and twigs, struck the match, and watched as the fire consumed her offering. Then stamped it out before it could move on to bigger, better things.

Paper was good. Letters were great.

She loved to lie on her stomach, the flames a breath away, her breath controlling them, guiding them. Her breath was the power that could flare up, her feet were the power that could stamp out, and her hands were the power that could ignite.

And no one knew.

Nothing remained of her small fires, except for a patch of scorched ground easily covered by grass cuttings, twigs, and leaves. No one used that lane behind the hedge anyway.

Until Simon moved in.

But that was then. This was now. This time tomorrow, she'd be boarding a plane at the Vancouver Airport. A few minutes after that, she'd be gone.

She felt her mother standing in the doorway, watching her pack. She knew she'd been standing there for some time, waiting for Chelsea to break the silence. Forget it, Mom, she wanted to say. I've nothing to say to you. Not unless you start something.

Jeans, shorts, shirts — everything neatly folded, placed inside the suitcase, checked off the list.

She hated being watched like this, feeling Mom's eyes boring into her back, making her head feel prickly, her legs tremble. Sooner or later something would happen. Simon would come home, the phone would ring, Mom would get the message and leave, or she'd finally break down and say something, to end the sticky silence. If she was waiting for Chelsea to make the first move she'd have a long wait.

"Have you got everything?"

Chelsea stiffened. When she spoke, her voice was bitter. "What do you care?"

"I do think it's for the best. We both need a rest from — "

"Oh, please. You want me gone." She turned and faced her mother. "Why did you ever keep me? I was a mistake. Why didn't you just erase me? You're the artist. A line here, a line there, gone. Fresh page, start again."

"Your father — "

"Oh, sure. Bring him into it." Chelsea gripped a T-shirt in her hand and gave her mother a twisted smile. "Got to hand it to you, though. You've picked the perfect solution. Why get a foster home in the same town when you can ship your kid to Dad, who just happens to live thousands of miles away. And this way is so beautiful. So like you. This way, you can get both Dad and me at the same time."

Her mother sighed. "Believe me, Chelsea, it's not like that at all."

"Oh. I should believe you now, should I?" She twisted the shirt until it was wound up as tightly as a rope.

"He's looking forward to having you. He's getting your room all fixed up . . . You'll love his house, it's got a stunning view. Chelsea, you're going to Hawaii! Most kids would kill to be in your shoes."

"You just don't get it, do you? Oh, what's the use? Don't you have something to do? Are you all packed for Bali?"

Her mother's jaw dropped. "How — ?"

"Didn't Simon tell you about our little chat? Simon tells me all sorts of things. Simon says — But you wouldn't want to hear that, would you? Might spoil your plans."

"That's enough!"

"Worked out really well, didn't it? Me going off to Dad's while you go off with Simon."

"Stop it or — " She raised her hand.

"Or you'll hit me?" Chelsea spread the rumpled T-shirt on her bed and smoothed out the wrinkles. "Why not? Why should anything be different now?"

Mom dropped her hand. "Oh, Chelsea. If you could only . . ."

Here it comes, Chelsea thought. The familiar refrain. If you could only be this or do that. Then what? Everything would be magically wonderful? We'd be a Disneyland mother and daughter team? Hardly.

"If you had a different attitude, if you could — "

"Well, I can't! Get it? So why don't you just go and let me finish packing. Go on, go!" Chelsea turned abruptly, folded her T-shirt, and placed it in the suitcase. Her mother walked out of the room, closing the door behind her.

Chapter 2

"Are we still on Earth?" Chelsea asked as they drove away from the Keahole-Kona Airport on the Big Island of Hawaii. "It looks like the ashpit of the universe."

Dad cleared his throat. "Welcome to the Land of Lava. A close cousin to . . . " he paused and hummed the familiar notes, ". . . the twilight zone."

Chelsea gave him a smile and a few points for trying.

She'd been surprised to see him waiting at the Honolulu Airport on Oahu. "Change planes at Honolulu," Mom had said. "Take an inter-island flight to the Big Island. Your dad will meet you there."

Wrong again, Mom. The thought gave her a small degree of satisfaction.

He had stood out among the crush of people, tall and lanky, hair still unruly, only now it was streaked with grey and the bushy beard she remembered had been shaved off. His tanned face broke into a huge grin when he saw her. "Chelsea! It's great to see you. How are you? How was your flight? Gosh, you've grown. Still those same dark eyes. And your hair's so long . . ." All the usual stuff.

After collecting her luggage, he stopped at a stand and bought a flowered lei. "Plumeria and hibiscus," he said, placing it around her neck. "I don't do this for just anybody." He leaned over to kiss her cheek.

Chelsea flinched and moved away. "Thanks."

If he was upset or surprised by her stiffness, he didn't show it. But she sensed a subtle change. On the flight to the Big Island he was quieter, more cautious. When he spoke, it was to point out something of interest. He hadn't asked her any questions, and certainly hadn't resumed his earlier heartiness.

Now, breathing in the fragrant blossoms of the lei, it struck her that maybe he was embarrassed, thinking they could pick up where they'd left off, seven years ago. Sure Dad, she thought. Dream on.

Soon they were out of the lava field, passing through small towns high above the sea. "There's a monument to Captain Cook down there," Dad said. He pointed to a bay rimmed by soaring bluffs. "He sailed in to repair a mast, and a fight broke out between his crew and the natives. He tried to end it and was killed. Can't see the monument today. Too hazy. You know about Captain Cook?"

"Yes," she said.

"You like history?"

"Yes." But more than history, she liked the beliefs that preceded it, the stories that were told to explain the world. It must have been a real twilight zone then, when people ventured into the Sky Kingdom and remained as stars, when gods walked upon the earth. When people could be rewarded for pleasing them and punished for making them angry.

The sky darkened. Within minutes rain was hammering on the roof of the car. "Tropical storm," said Dad. "Get them all the time, mostly on the east side of the island. It's real lush there, 'cause of all the rain. But the storms don't usually last long. Real sudden, real fierce, then over. And the rain's so warm. Took me a while to get used to it. High up, on Mauna Kea, you get snow. There's actually a short winter ski season, can you believe it? Great place, this. Bit of everything." He cleared his throat. "See those trees? Macadamia nuts. Real buttery and delicious. Kawena — she's my housekeeper — brought over a macadamia nut pie this morning, as a welcome for you."

Sometime after the rainstorm, somewhere past the macadamia nut orchard, they entered another stretch of lava. "Back to the twilight zone," said Dad.

Everything about this trip has a twilight zone feel to it, Chelsea thought. Being with Dad for one thing, after seven years of hardly a word. Sure, there were postcards from exotic places, the odd letter. Small gifts, mostly inappropriate — hadn't he realized she was no longer nine? — but easy to wrap and mail. Long-distance phone calls to wish her Happy Birthday and Merry Christmas, but never long enough to say anything.

But how much had she told him? *Dear Dad, How are you? I'm fine, school's fine, made the basketball team, won a poster contest, thanks for the new camera (that makes four now), got straight A's on my report card (lies, lies) . . .* What did he care, anyway? Why should he be interested in her? As the years passed he began to fade, turning misty and grey, disappearing into a real twilight zone, light-years away. Or might as well have.

Then there was this landscape, straight out of another world. It reminded her of a burnt chocolate cake. The road sliced through like a knife, straight, with the odd bump where things had bubbled up a little. It was definitely a B-grade land. Bubbled bumps, bleak and boring. Botched batter, burnt and black. A perfect landscape for her mood. Totally devastated, like her life.

It wasn't supposed to be like this. Mom wasn't supposed to give up on her, suddenly call Dad, and say, "Your turn. I can't handle this." *This* meaning Chelsea.

It had been Mom's idea to call her Chelsea because that's where it all began. In Chelsea, London, England. Hard to imagine Mom as a romantic. So her parents met in Chelsea. So she was conceived in Chelsea. So what?

So Dad could never stay in one place for more than a year. "That's what I love about your father," Mom used to say. "Every day's a new adventure."

Until every new adventure got tiresome. "He never wants to do what I want to do. Always traipsing through the bush with that wretched camera. What about my life? My art?" On and on until finally he packed up and left. Good-bye romance. Good-bye Dad. And when Chelsea became too much of an adventure, good-bye to her, too.

Strange that Mom, who was always harping on about the throw-away society, chanting "recycle, recycle" with every breath, thought nothing of throwing people out of her life. Except for Simon. He wasn't supposed to *be. Simple Simon met a pie man* . . . Trust Mom to fall for a nursery rhyme character. But there was nothing simple about him. Simon of the galleries, discovering new talent, dealing in priceless works of art. He was rich, successful, charming, clever — no, cunning was a better word. "If Simon fell in a sewer, he'd come up smelling of roses." That's what Dad used to say, when Simon organized his first photography shows, the ones that made him famous. But that was long ago when they were friends, before Dad moved away.

It wasn't supposed to be like this, having a near-stranger for a dad.

She noticed the way his fingers tapped the steering wheel, beating the rhythm of some silent tune. Noticed how he chewed his gum, his brow creased in thought, how he frowned sometimes, when he thought she wasn't looking. It struck her that it probably wasn't supposed to be like this for him, either.

"Chelsea, I was thinking . . . while you're here . . ." He stopped to clear his throat. "On the other hand, maybe it's too soon to make plans. Want some gum?" He fished inside his shirt pocket and offered her a pack of Trident.

"Thanks." She chewed in silence, thinking she ought to tell him to stop being so nervous. So what if they didn't talk? So what if they didn't get along? That was the normal family scene, as far as she was concerned. But then, wasn't that what Mom had planned?

Forget it, she said to herself. I'll make this work if it kills me. So there, Mom. I'll get this right.

Maybe she could even learn to talk to him again.

She smiled, pleased with the thought.

Kawena didn't waste time with hello, how are you. She loomed in the doorway, feet apart, hands on hips, and bellowed, "Where did you get that hair? It's straight from Tutu Pele herself."

"Now, Kawena," said Dad, "don't go filling her head with that nonsense."

Ignoring him, she lifted a handful of Chelsea's thick black hair and ran it through her fingers. "Twists and ropes and coils, shiny as lava. Pahoehoe hair." She looked into Chelsea's eyes, dark as her own. "Have you got a hot temper like Tutu Pele? Or do you take after your old man?" She slapped him fondly on the shoulder and lumbered towards her car. "See you Wednesday. And make sure Pahoehoe gets some of that pie. Don't you pig it all down yourself."

"She comes three days a week?" Chelsea asked as Kawena drove away.

"Don't worry," said Dad. "She likes you."

Chelsea wasn't worried. She was drawn to Kawena like iron filings to a magnet. Three afternoons a week they sat on the lanai overlooking the sea, drinking iced tea and telling stories. Chelsea told her the West Coast Native stories she'd read in school, stories about Raven the Trickster and how he created the world. In return, Kawena told her stories about Pele, the goddess of fire who boiled the rocks and sent torrents of lava down the flanks of Kilauea.

"Pele's driven from her homeland by her older sister, Na-maka-o-Kaha'i, goddess of the sea. She's in a jealous rage because Pele seduced her husband.

"So Pele comes, from the clouds blazing over Tahiti, across the ocean in a canoe, guided by her brother in the form of a great shark. From the land of Bora Bora to the islands of Hawaii.

"From one island to another she goes, digging deep pits to protect the sacred fires. She digs in Niihau, digs in Kauai, moving farther and farther along the island chain. And every time, her angry sister Na-maka-o-Kaha'i follows her and floods her pit with water. Finally, in Maui, they have a battle. A fierce battle between fire and water. And water is more powerful. The body of Pele is torn apart.

"But her spirit is free, and flees to the island of Hawaii. Here, at last, she finds a home." Kawena pointed to the peak rising in the distance. "On Mauna Loa, the largest mountain on Earth."

Something about Pele struck a chord with Chelsea. She pictured Pele's sister driving her away from home, much as Mom had driven her away. Was it possible that Mom had been jealous? Chelsea remembered the look on her mother's face when she had mentioned Simon's little chats. Maybe that was why she wanted Chelsea as far away as possible.

On nights when she couldn't sleep, or if the familiar nightmare woke her up, Chelsea sat on the lanai and looked down at the edge of the sea where the waves swept over the sand. The sound was soothing. Maybe, like Pele, she could find a home here. Without digging a pit and burying herself inside.

Most mornings, when Dad wasn't off taking pictures or working in the darkroom, they hiked along an old jeep trail, through the tall guinea grass, to a small black sand beach so secluded they considered it their own. Sometimes they left the beach and climbed over the rough lava to the site of an ancient temple. Looking over the stones at the sea pounding below, Chelsea thought about Kawena's stories of such ruins, where human sacrifices were made to the gods.

They spent hours swimming in the cove. Chelsea remembered her father as a powerful swimmer. Now, with his coaching, her own swimming improved. "Think I'm ready for the Ironman Triathlon?" she joked, completing her tenth lap from one end of the cove to the other. "I could do the swimming part, easy."

"We'd have to work on your running. You're awfully slow."

"Give me a break. You've got me swimming every spare second."

"Maybe it's time for a change. How about

cycling? We could work on that phase, build up to the 112 miles we need for the race, then do the running next month. Personally, I hate running."

"You do? So do I."

"Good. It's agreed then. Tomorrow we'll drive to Hilo and buy ourselves the best of all possible bikes."

"The kind that pedal themselves?"

"Good thinking! You must take after your dad."

Chelsea smiled happily. In the three weeks she'd been here, this was the first time he had acknowledged that he *was* her dad, not some distant relative forced to take her in. He hadn't even cleared his throat to say it.

Things were definitely looking up.

All she had to do was find some kids her own age. Not that a similar age guaranteed friendship — she knew that well enough — but she had to start somewhere. Maybe here she could make a fresh start, meet a kindred spirit, at least before school started in the fall. If not, there was always Kawena to talk to. And Dad.

His house was isolated, set on a hillside, surrounded by coconut palms, bright yellow hibiscus, and trailing clusters of red and purple bougainvillea. The best thing about it was its closeness to the beach. The worst thing, its distance from everywhere else. Though nothing on the Big Island was really that far away. In less than an hour they'd be in Hilo, shopping for bikes.

"Dad, do you think I could go to Kawena's village sometime and maybe meet some more people?"

"You're in luck! Kawena's invited us to a village luau this weekend."

"A what?"

"A luau. It's a feast. The star attraction is roast pig, specially cooked in an underground oven called an imu. They dig a pit, line it with — "

The car suddenly jerked.

"Dad! What's happening?" She clutched the door handle as the car wobbled and skittered to a stop.

"Sounds like a flat," he said, getting out to look. "Darn."

"Have you got a spare? Will it take long?"

"A few minutes." He opened the trunk and rummaged around for the jack. "Sit and relax, why don't you. Or explore the lava field."

Three weeks ago she would have balked at the thought of walking across what looked like one giant ashtray. Now she could see a certain beauty in the lava. She could tell the difference between the cindery *a'a* lava, and the glossy *pahoehoe*. And the lava fields weren't as bare as she'd thought. 'Ohelo shrubs flourished, bright with the red berries Pele was said to enjoy. Ferns grew through cracks and crevices, startling green against the black, especially after a rain when the sunshine made everything glisten.

Thinking of rain, she noticed the black clouds rolling in. Within seconds, rain started to fall. No sense rushing back to the car, she thought. Best to find shelter and wait it out.

There — wasn't that a lava tube? Dad had taken her to the one in Volcanoes National Park, a huge hollow tube formed by lava cooling and hardening on top, while continuing to flow underneath. This one was smaller, but dry. She crouched down and crawled inside.

And discovered she was not alone.

Chapter 3

Her eye caught a movement, the scrambling of something white. At least it's not a mongoose, she thought with relief. The ones she'd seen were light brown and slinky, like ferrets. What was it then? Her ears picked up a sound, the whimpering of some small animal. Could it be a puppy?

"Come on, fella." She strained her eyes in the dim light. Sure enough, a puppy scampered towards her, his tail practically wiggling off his backside. A warm bundle of fur tumbled into her lap. "How did you get here, Lava Dog?" The puppy licked her face. She giggled at the touch of his cold nose against her cheek.

Moments later the rain stopped. Chelsea crawled out of the lava tube with the puppy in her arms. "Did someone abandon you?" she wondered aloud. "Is that why you don't have a collar? But you look so healthy; someone took good care of you." She scratched the puppy behind his ears while he licked her hand. "Maybe someone had a flat tire and you wandered off. Is that what happened?" She hurried across the lava field, eager to show Dad. If it hadn't been for the flat tire, she wouldn't have found the puppy at all. What was that saying about clouds and silver linings?

Halfway back, she was surprised to see a woman walking towards her. She could see the road in the distance, and Dad's car, but there was no other car in sight. Strange, she thought. Where did the woman come from?

At least she thought it was a woman. She stopped, shielded her eyes against the sun, and blinked hard. For a moment the image appeared like a flame wavering in the heat, white-gold and flickery. She blinked again.

It was definitely a woman. She drifted across the lava, her feet barely touching the ground. Her long white skirt flowed loosely around her legs, her blonde hair rippled in the breeze. As she approached Chelsea she held out her arms. "You've found him!"

The puppy's ears pricked up. Before Chelsea could stop him, he scrambled into the woman's arms. "Guess he's yours," she said, trying to hide her disappointment.

"*Mahalo nui*," said the woman. "Thank you. I've been looking for a long time."

Maybe it was a trick of the light, the way a cloud suddenly shuddered across the sun, that changed the woman's face into a map of lines, creased and stained by wind, sun, and rain. Buried inside the folds were two black eyes rimmed with red, staring out as if from a fiery pit.

Chelsea shook her head, disturbed by the image. An old woman, that's all. White hair, not blonde. Eyes red from lack of sleep, worrying about her puppy.

She gave Chelsea a radiant smile. "Where did you find him?"

"In that lava tube." She looked over her shoulder and pointed. "How long was he — "

She turned back to the woman.

The woman was gone.

"Impossible," Chelsea muttered. "This doesn't happen. People don't vanish. Neither do dogs." But where could she have gone? There were no trees to hide behind. She couldn't have reached the road that quickly. But maybe she didn't go back to the road. Where then?

That crevice, half-hidden by 'ohelo shrubs? Was it large enough for a woman to duck inside? Possibly.

Or maybe she popped inside that lava tube beyond the crevice. That's what must have happened. Unless, of course, she really did vanish.

And that could mean only one thing.

Pele.

"Don't mess with Tutu Pele," Kawena had said. "And don't take anything that belongs to her."

She was upset when Chelsea showed her the pumice she'd brought back from the rim of the Kilauea Caldera. "You must return it to Tutu Pele," she said. "Otherwise, there's no telling what might happen."

"I've had enough bad luck already," Chelsea said. "What difference will this make?"

Kawena looked at her with sad eyes and shook her head.

Next day, Chelsea returned the pumice.

But Pele could be kind as well as vengeful. "If you're nice to Pele, she will reward you," Kawena said. "Sometimes people see her wandering along the roadside or across the lava. Sometimes she appears as an old hag. Even older than me, but maybe not so big," she chuckled. "Sometimes she appears as a beautiful young woman. Once she appeared to the lighthouse keeper. He invited her inside for some refreshments, they chatted, he said good-bye, and she disappeared. Whish! Like that! Next day, lava started to flow. Down, down, down the mountainside. Trees gone, houses gone, churches gone, beaches gone. And guess where Tutu Pele stopped the flow?"

"Right at the lighthouse?"

Kawena clapped her hands. "The very place! And we know why, don't we, Pahoehoe?"

And, Chelsea remembered as she continued across the lava, according to Kawena's stories Pele was often seen with a white dog.

She scanned the road, expecting to see her father. But he was nowhere in sight. Crouched down on the driver's side, probably, still fixing the tire. She felt a sudden chill. How long had she been gone? She hoped he wouldn't be angry. Not now, when they were beginning to feel comfortable with each other.

But then, Dad never did get angry. In three weeks she'd seen him nervous and awkward with her, impatient with the weather, annoyed at his camera, and excited about a million and one other things, chief of which was Kawena's macadamia nut pie. Never angry. Even before, when she was little, he never got angry. He just quietly left.

What would he think of her encounter with the mysterious woman? He liked to tease Kawena about her "Pele nonsense." Would he believe Chelsea or get mad at her for lying? She wished Pele had waited before disappearing, then Dad might have seen her and known Chelsea wasn't hallucinating or making up stories. But then again, maybe she had imagined it. The heat could do strange things to people. Maybe Kawena's stories were affecting her mind.

A black cloud covered the sun, and once again rain started to fall. She lowered her head and broke into a stumbling run, careful not to trip on the uneven surface. She didn't notice the jeep speeding down the hill towards her father's car. The sound of squealing tires made her look up, just in time to see the crash.

"You're sure you've got everything?" Kawena said. "Money, tickets, all that?"

Chelsea nodded. The last call for boarding had been made, so if she had forgotten anything it was too late now.

"You know what to do? Change planes at Honolulu — you've only got an hour to wait — then straight on to Vancouver, then over to Victoria. Your uncle will meet you at the Victoria Airport and take you home. It's all been arranged."

Home? Who was she kidding? This is your life, Chelsea Tennison. This is nothing unusual. Don't ever start to feel comfortable. Don't ever start to like something, or someone. Because in no time at all, it's ashes.

Kawena put an arm around her shoulder. "Oh, Pahoehoe. You're closed up tighter than an oyster. You sure there's nothing you want to say? Sometimes it helps to talk things out. Sometimes crying on the outside can make you feel a whole lot better inside."

Chelsea pressed her lips together. Her face was pale, her eyes cold. She remembered making an origami crane, carefully creasing and folding until the bird had a head, neck, tail, and wings.

She thought nothing could be more exquisite. Until she learned to make them smaller.

She thought she'd learned to fold her own feelings as tightly as they could go. Creases and folds, over and over. But each time, she discovered another fold was possible, no matter how tiny they became.

The creases had to be sharp, though. Nothing soft or rumpled. Hard-edged, that was the trick. The mistake she'd made in this current phase of her life was allowing a little corner to become unfolded. Allowing that origami crane to unfold a wing.

Never again would she allow that to happen.

So when Kawena hugged her and said, "Don't you worry, Pahoehoe, everything will be fine, we'll have a big luau for you when you come back," Chelsea shrugged her off, picked up her backpack, and walked to the plane without saying good-bye, without looking back.

PART 2

DIGGON

Chapter 4

Diggon was there the night they curbed the kid. When they forced open his mouth, wedged it against the concrete, stretched out his legs, and jumped on his head and back until —

Diggon was there, but he hadn't done anything.

He repeated the words, over and over, until they became a chant. *I didn't do anything, I didn't do anything*, the words a rhythm matching his footsteps, running at the sound of sirens, running through backyards and lanes and across the park, stopping only to puke in the bushes, running from streetlights and traffic lights and cops at every corner. *I didn't do anything*, but not able to escape the flashing light whirling red as blood in the back and front of his mind, whirling along with the voice screaming from somewhere deep inside —

But you let it happen.

Crouched beneath the dripping spruce in his own backyard, he threw up again and again until finally, exhausted, he leaned against the tree trunk, arms wrapped tightly around his chest, chanting, *oh God, oh God, what now . . .*

I shouldn't have run home. It's the first place they'll look. Maybe not tonight, but tomorrow.

Fear crawled along his veins, gnawed at his belly, throbbed in his head.

I didn't do anything.

But you let it happen.

I couldn't have stopped them.

You didn't try.

I couldn't have. Not against them.

Why were you with them in the first place?

They asked me. It was a party. It wasn't supposed to end like that.

He rubbed his arms, tried to control the shaking. If he hadn't gone to the mall, if he hadn't run into Blake and the others, if he'd stayed home instead of going to the party, if, if . . . But he couldn't undo it. This wasn't some video he could stop, rewind, eject, and switch for another. This was real.

So what now?

Nothing.

What about the kid? What if you killed him?

I didn't do anything.

They'll be after you for that, won't they? 'Cause you went out with that gang, big initiation night — admit it — and did nothing.

I didn't —

When they said jump, did you jump?
No.
*When they said kick pound smash, did you do
it?*
No.
So. Figure it out.

He couldn't stay here. Mom would know something was wrong and try to get it out of him. Dad
was too busy to notice, let alone care.

He couldn't — wouldn't — go to the cops.

What then?

He let himself into the house, no more quietly
than usual.

"Diggon?" Mom's voice, sleepy.

"Yeah. G'night, Mom."

In his room, Diggon grabbed his backpack,
stuffed in a flashlight, sleeping bag, and change of
clothes. Back downstairs, he opened the refriger-
ator so his parents would assume he was having
his usual snack. He rattled a few dishes and
pulled out a chair, scraping the floor as usual. He
put a couple of cans of Coke, a box of crackers,
and the jar of peanut butter into his pack. Then
opened the tea box where Mom kept extra cash
and put two twenty-dollar bills in his wallet.

He glanced at the notepad on the fridge door.
What do I say, good-bye? What's the use? They'll
know I've gone.

How about sorry about the kid?

Shut up about the kid.

What was his name?

*Shut up! I don't know his name, nobody knew
his name, he was just there, in the wrong place at
the wrong time.*

He drank a glass of water and wiped the sweat
off his forehead, wondering how he could possibly
be sweating when he felt so cold.

A sudden impulse made him scrawl across the
notepad, *Gone camping with CJ.* Summer holidays, no school to worry about, he'd gone camping with CJ before. They'd figure he was spend-
ing the night at CJ's and getting an early start
tomorrow. They wouldn't miss him till Monday
night at the earliest.

Won't they miss the peanut butter?

No, I'm the only one who eats the stuff.

Maybe the money?

Just get out of here.

He opened the kitchen door and crept outside,
pulling up his collar and hunkering down inside
his jacket. It was a few minutes after midnight.
With any luck he'd hitch a ride with a trucker
and be at the ferry terminal for the first sailing.
Then to the island, then to the basin, then to the
safety of the cove. With any luck he'd be there by
noon.

Why should you have any luck?

That voice again.

Because I breathe. Because I'm Diggon.

Not anymore, hounded the voice. *Diggon was curbed tonight, along with that kid. Diggon is gone. You're nothing. You're nobody now.*

Chapter 5

But he had been somebody. A skinny, brown-haired, wide-eyed kid, content to go his own way. Having the gift of stillness as Gran used to say.

"A good, independent worker," his report cards always said. "Prefers to work alone."

Why did those comments sound so negative? he wondered. "Quiet and reflective." Like it was some kind of disease. "Does not take part in group activities."

"Why not?!" Dad blasted him as usual. "Join in. Be a team player. You've got to be part of the group. You'll never make it otherwise, Diggon."

Why had that name stuck? Funny how he'd grown into it, how easily he'd worn it. Gran had started it, by giving him a set of gardening tools for his fourth birthday. Rake, hoe, shovel, and trowel. Digging into a patch of dirt, he discovered gold coins, and from that moment he was hooked.

Later, he realized she had pre-planted the foil-covered chocolate coins, but by then it didn't matter. There were other treasures in the earth, other reasons for digging: worms to take out, seeds to put in, secret tunnels and hiding places to create.

It didn't bother Dad, then, that Diggon wasn't a team player. "That's our boy," he'd say proudly. "Never have to worry about amusing him. He just keeps digging and digging."

A two-year-old cousin babbled "Diggon" and gave him the name.

Now he felt as if that part of him was gone.

Shivering in the rain, he set off along the highway, holding out his thumb at the approach of any vehicle. It could be dangerous, but he wouldn't take unnecessary chances. If anyone tried anything he'd jump out no matter how fast they were going. Anyway, he had his knife.

Gran had given it to him on his tenth birthday, five years ago. "It belonged to your grandpa," she said. "He had the gift of stillness, too. Would sit for hours, turning a chunk of wood into something beautiful. Like that heron on our mantle you like so much, carved from yellow cedar. Your grandpa carved it the summer we bought Heron Cove." She closed the blade and placed the knife in Diggon's hand. "Try it," she had said. "Make something out of nothing. Make the wood sing."

He patted his pocket to make sure that the

knife was still there.

Oh, smart.

The voice again.

Yeah, so I've always got my knife. You've got to have something to protect yourself. Especially at night, hitchhiking.

Smart. After what you've done, you're prepared to pull a knife on someone?

I didn't do anything.

You've dug yourself a real hole, Diggon.

"Shut up!" He pressed his hands to the sides of his head to blot out the pain, to stop the voice, but it kept on and on, rolling like the wheels swishing over the pavement. *Try and climb out of it this time. Try and climb out of it this time.*

PART 3

BETH

Chapter 6

"Hey, Fish-breath! Any love letters?"

"Yes!" Beth ran up the stairs, hugging the mail to her chest. "So ha, ha, Mealworm. You can't gloat today."

"Watch it!" Field flung out an arm as Beth's foot brushed against the pile of hockey cards and scattered them over the porch. "I just finished sorting them, you — !"

"Sor-ree." She bolted through the door. "Mom! Mail's here!"

She shuffled through the envelopes, congratulating herself on not rising to her brother's bait. Of course there weren't any love letters. No letters from Vancouver, period. But it was summer holidays, so he could write from another place, like Calgary, where his grandmother lived. Maybe he —

What was this? A letter postmarked Hawaii, of all places. Maybe he was there on a holiday?

But of course it wasn't from him. It was addressed to her father, R. Tennison. No way could that R. be mistaken for a B. But it was from a law firm, and his dad was a lawyer, so maybe —

Give it up, Beth. Give up on him, period.

She left the mail on the kitchen counter and went to her room, kicking aside the piles of school stuff she had to sort out or throw away. Dog-eared notebooks, crumpled tests, gym strip that could practically jog on its own, pencils chewed into a variety of toothy patterns, a seed collage demonstrating the principles of something important, she couldn't remember what. She still had packing to do too, since tomorrow they were leaving Victoria for Tidewater, their summer home on Goodridge Basin. Would it be the same though, this summer?

No. She dumped that thought into the waste-basket, along with the year's accumulated left-overs, and started to empty her drawers.

She chose the underwear drawer first, because tucked away at the back, underneath the bras and panties, was her diary. And the letters. Hiding them there had been nothing short of brilliant. That drawer would be the last place her brother would look.

He hadn't always been so finicky. Even now, three years later, she cringed at the memory of him with that bra on his head.

It was a special outing with Mom. Afternoon tea at the Empress Hotel, then shopping for her first bra. They were in the lingerie department at Eaton's, looking things over, when a familiar voice suddenly hollered, "Here's one, Beth! Is this the right size?"

She froze, totally humiliated. He was supposed to be with Dad! Somewhere else! But no, there he was — with a black bra, size 80 if anything, strapped to his head with the cups perked over his ears.

"How about this one?" he yelled. In case she hadn't heard him the first time.

The way she remembered it, everyone in the store turned and pointed at her twenty-eight-inch chest, snickering, "Maybe in ten years."

She had sunk behind a rack of fleecy robes, longing for death.

Field was ten now, and the thought of touching his fifteen-year-old sister's underwear was enough to make him throw up. Too bad she hadn't thought of this hiding place sooner, before he'd discovered the diary on her bookshelf and the letters in her atlas. On the page showing Vancouver of all places. How could she have been so stupid! So totally obvious!

After his discovery, Field had locked himself in the bathroom and read the letters out loud so the whole street could hear. Worse, he'd read pages from her diary.

"He did!" she had cried, choking with rage. "All my stuff from last summer, with the window open, too!"

"Calm down," said Mom. "Nobody heard a thing. Field's voice isn't even — "

"I'll kill him!" She broke away from her mother and flung herself at Field, knocking him over with such force he struck his head against the edge of the sink and needed to be rushed to the hospital for stitches.

I ought to give him another scar for bringing up the letters, Beth thought.

But it was always like that. Just when she figured she was over it, someone would say something, or she'd see something, and there he'd be, back in her mind. Stirring up her thoughts, tripping somewhere between her heart and her belly, making her sick with wanting. "Oh Mom," she cried, that last day at Tidewater, "I hurt."

"I know," said Mom. "I'm so sorry." And later, when the letters stopped coming, "There'll be other loves in your life. Each one will become a part of you. I know, I know," she added, holding Beth close, "it doesn't make it any easier now."

Six months had passed since the last letter. Ten months since she'd seen him. She remembered it so clearly, that end-of-summer night at Tidewater.

The fire was dying down. Her parents had packed up the jars of mustard and relish, the remaining wieners and buns, and assorted debris, and headed back to the cabin with Field in tow. "Why can't I stay," he whined. "*He's* staying. Beth's staying."

"Not for long," said Dad. "Got that, you two? And don't forget to douse the fire."

But instead of dousing the fire, they added more wood, stirred it to a blaze, and snuggled in closer.

Waves lapped the shore, like longings. The sky was bright with stars. Electric. Tonight, Beth thought, something wonderful will happen. "This is my favourite place in the world," she said softly. "I wish I could stay here forever."

He brushed against her arm and said something. But his words were lost in a shower of sparks.

"You're what?" She couldn't have heard right.

"Moving to Vancouver. Our house in Victoria's up for sale."

"But you'll still come here for holidays, won't you? Next summer?"

He shook his head. "Too far, Dad says. Too much hassle, getting on and off the island every weekend. He wants to sell the cabin, too."

Something twisted sharply inside her. "You can't! You just — "

It happened so quickly. Right there, in mid-sentence, he leaned over and kissed her lightly on the mouth. Then he drew back, smiling the smile that sent shivers down her spine and curled the backs of her knees. She sat quietly, holding onto the silence, holding onto the delicious throbbing she felt inside, in a part of her she hadn't known existed. Holding onto this perfect, perfect moment.

When they moved forward to kiss again, their noses bumped. Gently, he touched her face, tilted it slightly, drew it close. She closed her eyes, melted into the long, slow kiss, and let him wrap himself around her.

Now she lay on her bed with his letters and wrapped herself up in the memory of that night. Would she ever be that happy again? Tears stung the corners of her eyes and slid down into her ears. Was it possible to get over it, ever?

Chapter 7

The news of Chelsea's coming burst into the room. "When's she coming? And why?"

"What does she look like? How long's she staying?"

"What if she doesn't like us?"

"Of course she'll like us," said Field. "We're cousins. Her *only* cousins."

"She might not like you," his sister pointed out. "Being younger and being a boy. Not to mention ugly."

"What about you, Zit-face! You'll bore her to death."

Beth knew he was teasing, but his words hurt. She was afraid he might be right.

When she tried to look at things through Chelsea's eyes, everything came up boring. She hated the thought of Chelsea sneering at her, at her home and family, making them small and insignificant. But how could two school teachers match up with a world-famous photographer and a former model as parents? How could Tidewater match up with the swaying palms and pounding surf of Hawaii? Even though Tidewater was on the beach, the water was too cold for a tropical sort of person like Chelsea.

Who was she, this cousin? No one knew her, or anything about her, except that she was the only child of Dad's only brother whom he never heard from. Unless you could count the Christmas card greeting. "I am fine and hope you are too." No post-and-brag newsletters from Uncle Mark. But then, he didn't need to brag. They often saw his name on film credits, National Geographic stuff, mostly. He took unnecessary risks, according to Dad, specializing in natural disasters like volcanoes.

When she was younger, Beth had used him to gain status amongst her classmates. "My Uncle Mark, you know, the famous photographer? He lives in Hawaii and we're going there during the holidays." But when her friends started to say, "Sure, Beth, like you went last year and the year before. Tell us another one," she stopped talking about him altogether.

Then there was Chelsea's mother, Alison. "From a wealthy family in England," Dad had said. "Had her own apartment in London, worked as a model. That's how she met Mark — he was photographing her for some fashion magazine.

That's before he specialized in other disasters. Before that, she'd gone to art school and had her own exhibition before she was twenty-one. Spoiled rotten, got whatever she wanted. Still can't figure why she wanted my brother. There's no accounting for taste."

Is that what Chelsea is like? Beth wondered. Gorgeous and talented? Spoiled? Unbelievably cool? She felt small just thinking about it.

Not that she wasn't unbelievably cool herself. Well, maybe not that cool. She certainly wasn't gorgeous. But her face wasn't that bad, in spite of what Field said. Only — she counted carefully — seven zits. True, she hadn't been the most popular girl in Grade 9, but she had her share of friends. And Grade 10 might be different.

She wore the right clothes, liked the right music, watched the right movies. She was invited to sleep-overs and birthdays and skating parties and she giggled and talked about boys and laughed too loudly and did silly things to get their attention, like everyone else. She was open and honest and shared confidences about everything — except about *him*. He remained a secret. Like the danger game. And Tidewater itself.

Beth loved their summer home, the green shade of cedar and fir, the starflowers and tiger lilies, the trumpety orange flowers of honeysuckle and the hummingbirds they attracted. She loved the beach, even if it was barnacly and the water icy cold. She didn't mind the clammy reek of low tide. She loved rowing across the basin, spotting seals. She loved digging for clams, jigging for cod, making huckleberry pies. The sun bleached her hair honey-blonde, and she tanned "brown as a berry," as Dad said. When she laughed, her green eyes sparkled.

At Tidewater, Beth was truly herself. She didn't have to play the part of Teenage Wannabe. She could just *be*. There were no other kids around, just her and Field and *him*. The three of them formed a unit, a bond.

Or had. It would be different this summer, without him.

And now there was Chelsea.

"According to this letter," Dad explained, "Chelsea was with Mark at the time of the accident. Her mother, Alison, is off backpacking in Indonesia, no one knows where. So until she comes back, or until Mark is out of the woods, Chelsea's staying with us." He took off his glasses and rubbed his eyes. "That's so typical of my brother."

Mom glanced over the lawyer's letter. "You had no idea you were Chelsea's guardian? Mark never told you? Or asked?"

"Not a word. Of course I don't mind — *we* don't mind — but wouldn't you think he'd let me know? Typical. He just plows ahead following his own course, never a thought for anybody else. As for Alison — wouldn't you think she'd keep in touch with her own daughter?"

"Poor kid," said Mom. "Imagine what she's going through. She doesn't know where her mother is, doesn't know how long her dad will be in a coma or what state he'll be in when he comes out of it. And she doesn't have a clue about us. She knows as much about us as we know about her."

"She's in for a shock."

Mom grinned. "I'll say. We're so normal."

"Boring's more like it," said Field. "Especially Beth."

"Oh, come on," Dad said. "Chelsea's just a year older, they'll get along like a house on fire. Won't you, Beth?"

Beth didn't answer. Dad knew kids well enough to know it wouldn't be that simple. But getting along like a house on fire? What a stupid expression. A house on fire burned down, leaving a smouldering mess of charcoal and ashes. Not a nice image for friendship.

PART 4

TIDEWATER

Chapter 8

For the first few days, Chelsea didn't speak. Except for please, thank you, good night, I'm fine.

"She's still in shock," Mom said. "Give her time."

"She's not a bit like I imagined," said Beth. "She's so — I don't know — invisible, the way she hovers around the edges and stares off into space. It's like she goes into a trance." At the same time, Beth had to admit, there was a presence about her cousin that commanded attention. She had pictured Chelsea looking the way her name sounded, blonde, blue-eyed, and bubbly. Instead, she was dark and silent. Even bewitching.

The word made her laugh. Get real, Beth. She's your sixteen-year-old cousin, not some flipping *star*. "I wish she'd act more normal. Like talk, or smile, even. She never smiles, unless that twitching of her mouth is a smile. And have you noticed her eyes? They're so huge and round and black. Those gold flecks in them give me the creeps. They look like they're going to reach out and pull you in."

"Cool!" Field exclaimed. "Take a video and send it to that TV program."

"She hardly eats a thing," Beth went on. "Have you noticed how she picks at her food? Even pizza! And how come she's always wearing shirts with those long baggy sleeves? It's hot out! I don't get it! And she makes snuffling noises at night, like a rodent." That's better, she thought. Bring her down to earth.

But then she felt guilty. Knowing Chelsea was unhappy. Not knowing how to help.

Chelsea may not have spoken, but she listened and watched. And tried to sleep through the nightmare.

It was always the same. A faceless figure, the muggy smell of heat. Someone finding her, hiding under the covers. Someone smothering her cries, sounds strangling in her throat. She woke, choking, fighting for breath. Afraid of the darkness, longing for light, for the bright explosion of flame.

On the first morning she had gotten up early and waited while Uncle Rob called the hospital. "Still the same," he said. "A fractured leg, lacerations. He's lucky to be alive. At least he's out of the coma. They're doing everything they can," he added gently. She nodded, but said nothing.

"Come on, Chelsea," Aunt Carolyn said. "Breakfast on the verandah. Best time of the day."

She followed her aunt outside and took her place at the table, facing the wild tangles of honeysuckle that shaded the verandah. Sunlight shone through the leaves, bathing everything in green-tinted light.

"Chelsea," said Uncle Rob, "you're taking part in a family tradition. Your dad and I used to have breakfast at this very same table when we were kids." His round, friendly face cracked in a smile. For the first time, Chelsea noticed his greyish-blue eyes were the same colour as her dad's.

"Probably ate the same yucky stuff," said Field, eyeing his father's plate. "Whoever heard of putting peanut butter on pancakes?"

Beth glanced at Chelsea. "Dad's big on family tradition."

"Except for the outhouse," Field said. "We don't have to keep using that, at least. Unless you really want to keep up the tradition. Do you, Chelsea?"

She shrugged and rearranged the pancakes on her plate. It didn't matter one way or another. She didn't care.

After breakfast she would walk. Across the lawn, through the gate of the white picket fence, along the narrow path through the meadow. Salt flats really, Aunt Carolyn had said, but everyone called it the meadow. It was bristly with sea grass and littered with driftwood washed up by the high winter tides. At the edge of the meadow she crossed the wooden bridge over the slough, and from there made her way to the beach.

She walked along the beach to the wharf, where her uncle moored his cabin cruiser. Then she turned and walked back, past the bridge, past the boathouse, all the way to the spit.

After her walk, she sat against a log or the boathouse and stared out at the basin, a near-perfect circle ringed by gentle hills. She wondered how the water could stay so calm. Didn't it ever get stormy? She didn't break her silence to ask.

Sometimes, she took her journal out of her backpack and made sketches of the cabin, the meadow, the beach, to show Dad whenever, *if* ever, she had the chance.

On the third morning, Uncle Rob had let her speak to the doctor. "The fractured leg should heal in twelve weeks," he had said. "The coma situation, though . . . " Dad had been in a coma for four days. The doctor explained that if a person was in a coma longer than forty-eight hours there was a 50–50 chance he would have a complete physical recovery. And a 50–50 chance he could have "severe emotional disturbances." He went on to talk about social withdrawal and low frustration tolerance but Chelsea shut him out. A

50–50 chance, was that good or bad? Would Dad be able to have her back? What did a 50–50 chance mean for her?

Then there was the memory loss. Dad couldn't remember what happened after the accident. He couldn't remember continuous events from day to day. "We're working on it," the doctor had said. "He's a very strong, very determined man. You'll be speaking to him yourself in a few days, I'm sure. Write to him as often as you can. Let him know how you're doing, that's the ticket."

Would he remember this place? she wondered. *Tidewater*. She wrote the title at the top of a page and started cross-hatching her drawing of the cabin. It had been built way back in the forties, Uncle Rob had explained, and stuccoed with an unusual mixture of plaster and bits of broken clam shells, coloured glass, and stones. Strange that Dad had spent his summers here as a boy but had never talked about it. Not that she could remember.

She turned to another page and drew a rough map of the area, trying to connect what lay in front of her with what she'd seen on the big map in the cabin. Goodridge Basin was almost completely round, with little bays and coves tucked away out of sight. At the end of Billings Spit, where she walked every day, there was a narrow passage where the basin emptied into the harbour. Or was it the other way around?

The land across the water was a peninsula. "East Bracken," her uncle had said, "as opposed to Bracken, the town on this side of the basin." It was across the water that Field and Beth rowed every day, disappearing behind a point called Hill Head. What was the attraction over there? Chelsea wondered. But only for a moment. She didn't really care.

She shaded in the water of the basin and harbour, wishing she'd brought her coloured pencils. At the far end of the harbour there was another spit. She couldn't see it, but remembered it from the map. What was it called, Whiffle, Whitten? No, Whiffen Spit. How could she forget? Uncle Rob always made the same sound effects when he mentioned it. Whiff and spit. It jutted out like a crooked finger, almost closing the entrance to the harbour. That's where the tide ripped through like crazy, Beth said. Where they weren't allowed to row.

Beyond that was Juan de Fuca Strait, separating Vancouver Island from Washington State. When Chelsea walked to Billings Spit and along the beach to the mouth of the river, she could see the Olympic Mountains, etched sharply against the sky.

When she grew tired of sketching, she scribbled down thoughts or fragments of poems. Sometimes she filled the page with questions, written in huge bubble letters. Like, *WHY?* Or,

Will it ever end? And sometimes, in minuscule letters, *everything will be all right.*

She never wrote about daily events in her journal, but kept things pressed inside. Memories small enough to be protected by the pages. Memories big enough not to need words. Like the seven-year-old crane with all its folds, so crumpled she'd never be able to smooth it out. And a pressed plumeria flower from the lei Dad had given her, brown around the edges, but still fragrant.

When a postcard arrived from Bali, via Hawaii, she looked at the glossy procession of dancers winding their way through rice paddies, read the printed blurb about the oldest dance-drama on the island, but didn't bother to read her mother's message. Instead, she tore the postcard into small fragments and dropped them into the wood-burning stove.

"Wasn't that from your mom?" Aunt Carolyn asked. "How's she doing?"

Chelsea shrugged. Nothing Mom scrawled on a postcard would make any difference.

Every afternoon her cousins rowed across the basin. She remained on the beach and listened to the splash of oars, the rumbly creak of oarlocks. Sometimes, their voices drifted back to her. Sometimes, she caught her name. She knew they were talking about her, wondering about her. She didn't care.

Once, when she was little, Dad had taken her rowing. Where was it? Some lake where they'd rented a cabin for a holiday. Mom came too, and for a while it was fun. They sang "Row Row Row Your Boat" as a round in three parts, and everything was fine until Chelsea decided she wanted to row. After she and Dad traded seats, he put his hands over hers, rowing along with her until she got the idea. "Both together, that's the key. OK?"

He took his hands away. But her left hand was weaker than her right and the boat kept going in circles.

"Harder on the left," Dad said patiently, while Mom, in the bow, muttered about how she wanted to get back before tomorrow.

Chelsea tried to pull harder on the left, but she lost her grip and the oar slipped out of the oarlock.

"Oh wonderful," Mom said, annoyed. "Isn't this just wonderful."

Chelsea leaned out to grab the oar. In her eagerness to reach it, she knocked over the oarlock. She wailed as it flipped over the side and out of sight.

Mom scowled and lifted the oarlock out of the water. "It's tied on anyway!"

By now the oar had floated away. Dad had to dive in and swim for it.

"Why didn't you just use the other oar and

paddle after it?" Mom complained when he climbed back in, dripping wet.

She glowered at Chelsea, but she didn't need to. Chelsea knew it was her fault the day was spoiled. Why couldn't she have just sat there? Why had she insisted on rowing the boat? Why couldn't she get things right? There was no more "merrily merrily" that day.

Watching her cousins row back across the basin, Chelsea realized that was the last time her family had done anything together.

She was surprised then, at the end of the first week, to hear herself ask, "Could you teach me to row?"

Eyes flicked around the table. Raised eyebrows, tentative smiles. "Sure," Beth said. "No problem. We can row somewhere and have a picnic lunch." She grinned at her mother. Finally! They'd been tiptoeing around as if Chelsea were made of glass. Maybe now they could relax.

After breakfast, Field ran off to the boathouse to collect the oars and life jackets, while Mom bustled about the kitchen making sandwiches. "You want to grab some apples, Beth? Don't forget the cookies."

"How about some fishing?" Dad suggested. "You want to try that too, Chelsea? Your luck can't be any worse than mine."

Chelsea's mouth twitched and she shook her head.

"Ready?" Beth grabbed her pack. "See you," she called to her parents. "We won't be long."

"Take as long as you like," said Dad. "It's a beautiful day, not a breath of wind."

"You have to be careful in the basin," Beth explained as she led the way across the meadow. "Sometimes the wind whips up out of nowhere. It gets really rough with whitecaps and then — whoa! It's really hard to row. I hate it when it's rough."

"Hurry up, you guys." Field had dragged the rowboat to the water and was waiting with the life jackets.

"Sit in the middle, Chelsea," Beth said as they clambered in. She pushed off with an oar, then sat in the stern. "I'll show you from here."

Field perched in the bow. "I'll keep a lookout so you don't have to keep turning around, OK?"

"Thanks."

"No logs, nothing ahead."

Beth leaned forward, ready to begin the coaching. "Good, you're holding the oars right. Move your arms forward and back. It's weird because you're moving ahead by looking backwards. See what I mean? The oars have to slice through the water at the same time. Pull them both together. If you just pull on one oar, you go around in circles."

"Try it," said Field.

"I'll probably do it without trying." Chelsea leaned forward at the waist and pulled back, concentrating on keeping both arms together.

"No logs, nothing ahead."

"Once you get the rhythm it's easy," Beth said. "Move back, and the oars cut through the water and push the boat forward. Move forward, lift the oars, and the boat glides — you hope."

The boat slid along in a rhythm of splashes and circles as the oars dipped below the surface and arched above it. Soon Chelsea could forget about the movement of her arms. She watched the sunlight glinting off the water and the wake of silvery bubbles. Now that she was actually in the basin, she could make out all sorts of dips and bites in the shoreline. On the far side of Hill Head she could see crescent-shaped beaches, rocky points, even a small island. She could add that to her map later.

"You've got it!" Beth gave her a pleased grin. "You're doing great!"

"No logs, nothing ahead."

"Give it a rest, Slug-brain. There won't be any logs or rocks this far from shore."

"There *could* be, Fish-breath. You don't know everything."

"Where should we go?" Chelsea asked.

"We usually go to that island," said Field. "See, in the cove? It's called Deadman's Island because — "

"Not always." Beth's voice was unexpectedly sharp. "I mean, we don't always go there." She glared at her brother. The last thing Chelsea needed to hear was "dead man." Not with her dad barely out of a coma and still listed in critical condition. And, she admitted to herself, there was a more selfish reason for cutting off her brother. She considered the island and the cove *her* territory. She wasn't sure she wanted to share it with Chelsea. At least, not yet.

"I don't care where we go," Chelsea said. "Anybody else want to row?"

"Nah," said Beth. "Let's drift for a while."

Chelsea didn't argue. She slid the oars into the boat, content to let it drift. The basin was smooth as glass. She felt herself drifting away when she gave a sudden start. "Look! A dog! But it can't be, can it? Not in the middle of the basin."

Her cousins laughed. "It's a seal, what else!"

The seal twitched his whiskers and stared at them. "He comes up all the time," said Field. "Don't you, boy?"

The seal flipped over, splashed his tail, and disappeared beneath the surface.

"He'll come back, just wait."

Within seconds the seal popped up again.

"Let's follow him," said Chelsea, pulling on the oars. But as she approached, the seal disappeared.

A sudden splash, and there he was again. "He's right behind me," Beth exclaimed. "I can see him under the water."

The seal popped up first on one side of the boat, then on the other. Sometimes he glided underneath, rolling over so close to the surface they could make out the markings on his skin. "Look where he's heading," said Field.

Straight to Deadman's Island.

Chapter 9

"In here, Chelsea. Go hard on the left so you'll turn."

She rowed towards the small beach facing the cove. As soon as they heard the crunch of gravel they climbed out, leaving Field to tie up the boat.

"Make sure you tie it up good," said Beth.

"I did. Have you got the pack?"

"Yeah, come on. We'll go to the grassy side and have lunch." She hurried them up the rocky slope to a small clearing, sheltered by firs and a scraggly arbutus. A few scorched rocks marked the remains of a campfire.

"Someone's been here," Field said eagerly. "Hey Beth, maybe it's — "

"Get real," she said. "Those same rocks were here yesterday, remember? They've been here since last summer." She took a long look at the cove, not daring to hope. But there was no sign of life.

She followed the others to the far side of the island overlooking the basin. They sat on the sun-bleached grass while she opened her pack and passed around cookies and sandwiches.

"You could slide straight into the water from here," said Field, taking a bite of his cookie.

"Go right ahead," said Beth.

"Well, we did it once," he said indignantly. "You thought it was fun, then. But of course we know why." He spoke in a singsong voice, needling her. "Remember that time when — "

"Shut up."

"Bet Chelsea wants to know," he said. "Don't you, Chelsea?"

Beth pushed him in the shoulder. "I said, shut up!"

"Fish-breath!" he taunted, shoving back.

"Hey!" The urgency in Chelsea's voice stopped them. "Isn't that your boat?"

They followed her gaze, stunned to see the rowboat drifting away from the island. "You idiot, Field!" Beth snapped. "I told you to tie it up."

"I did! You should've checked it, you're so smart. Now what are we going to do?"

"Won't the seal bring it back?" Chelsea asked. Her cousins gave her a blank look, not sure if she was kidding. "No? Guess someone'll have to swim for it."

"What?" Field squawked. "It's miles away. And that water's freezing. Start yelling or something. Someone'll hear."

"How come you're such a chicken all of a sudden?" Beth said. "If this was a danger game you'd be after that boat in a minute."

"Well it isn't, is it? So why don't you shut up or get it yourself!"

Beth was close to tears. "It's your fault! You didn't tie it up!"

They were so busy arguing they didn't notice Chelsea poised on top of a rock at the island's edge. Suddenly, there was a loud splash.

"Chelsea!" Beth raced towards the rock. "Come back! You'll never make it!"

"Help!" Field screamed, running after her. "Someone with a boat, help!"

"Shut up! There's no one around to — "

"You've really done it, Beth. You're going to — "

"What do you mean, I've done it? You didn't tie it up!"

"What if she isn't that good a swimmer?" Field hopped from one foot to the other, frantic. "She's used to Hawaii water, you know, not this cold water. What if she gets that hyper thing?"

"You're the hyper thing! Would you shut up!"

"And she just finished eating. What if she gets a cramp? What if she doesn't make it?"

But she *was* making it. Beth stared, amazed. Each powerful stroke took Chelsea closer to the boat. Nothing seemed to bother her, not the cold, not the distance, nor the fact she was fully clothed.

"She's really cool, isn't she?"

Beth didn't answer. She couldn't help but be impressed. At the same time, she felt a twinge of jealousy. Why couldn't she have done it? The admiration in her brother's voice made it even worse.

She watched as Chelsea reached the boat, pulled herself up, shook the water out of her hair, and wrung out her shirt as best she could. Then she picked up the oars and rowed back, with no apparent effort.

"You're some swimmer," Field exclaimed, wading out to meet her. "Wow!"

The corners of her mouth twitched in what might have been a smile. "My dad taught me."

"I'll row back," said Field. "You want to be lookout this time?"

"Sure," Chelsea said. She moved up to the bow, breathing hard.

Good, Beth thought. At least she's human.

"A wiener roast tonight?" Field bounced up and down with excitement. "Why?"

"To celebrate Chelsea's rescue of the boat," his mother said. "Although we shouldn't let you come." She scowled at him. "That was very careless."

"Mom, I said I was sorry."

"Well then, hustle up and get some newspaper and matches for the fire. Come on, girls. Help carry this stuff." She loaded them with wieners and buns, ketchup, mustard, and relish, drinks, and potato salad, and they all trooped down to the beach.

At the beginning of the summer, Beth explained, they collected planks and driftwood to build a windbreak, a bench, and a table for picnics and wiener roasts. "Another family tradition. Or ritual, whatever."

"We do it every year," Field added. "Every summer we get it just perfect, then every winter it gets washed away by storms and high tides."

"And every year Dad swears we're never going to bother again," Beth laughed.

"We've even got a place for the fire." Field proudly pointed out the well-defined circle of stones, scorched by previous fires.

There was a ritual to the fire, too. Chelsea watched as Field crumpled newspaper and placed it inside the circle of stones. He laid sticks and twigs on top, crisscrossing one way, then the other, leaving air spaces in between. Her fingers tingled when he struck the match. An urge roared up inside, an urge so powerful she wanted to tear the match from his hand and set things blazing herself. But she held back.

She watched him light the paper, watched it curl and blacken as the flame ate its way to the kindling. When that began to crackle, he added chunks of bark and larger pieces of wood. Chelsea helped, careful not to smother the flames.

Chapter 10

Diggon arrived at Heron Cove late that afternoon. After leaving home he had hitched a ride with a trucker, spent the night huddled outside the ferry terminal, and boarded the Queen of Saanich for the first sailing. It had taken forever to get to the cove, short rides from here to there, long waits in between. In Victoria he went into a grocery store and bought some cookies and a bag of chips. He scanned the morning paper, expecting to see his name blaring across the headlines, MICHAEL SPENCE, KNOWN AS DIGGON, WANTED. But there was nothing.

Because you're not in Vancouver. The voice broke into his thoughts. *That's where the headline will be, in the Vancouver paper. That's where they'll show your picture, tell what you did.*

I didn't do anything.

He waited for another ride, thumb out, face blank. At least it wasn't raining. But it was warm and getting warmer. Almost stifling.

I didn't do anything.

Finally a car stopped. He got in and nodded his thanks. He stared out the window, trying not to think.

He leaned over in the passenger seat, buried his face in his hands, and groaned. The driver stopped and let him out, afraid he might be sick in the car.

The next ride took him as far as the turn-off to East Bracken. He got out, mumbled his thanks, and waved off the driver's "Have a nice day."

Not likely.

He decided to walk the rest of the way, a wise decision since there was little traffic. He walked along the narrow road that circled Goodridge Basin, rising and falling, twisting and turning through the woods, in and out of sunlight. One mile after another until finally he turned down the remote dirt road that led to the cabin at Heron Cove.

At least Dad hadn't sold it. Everything was the way they'd left it on Labour Day, ten months ago. He checked windows and doors but found nothing disturbed. The cabin key and shed key were still carefully hidden. The sixteen-foot aluminum runabout was beside the shed, turned over for the winter. Even his tunnel, cut into the broom bushes growing on top of the bank, was the way he had left it, the opening perfectly concealed. A few yellow flowers, left over from spring, clung to the branches. It looked safe and inviting.

He decided against going into the cabin, preferring his own sanctuary. He crawled inside the tunnel and spread out his sleeping bag. Through the bushes, he could see the cove, the dock, the island, and the basin. Anyone coming over the water, he would see. Anyone coming down the driveway, he would hear. Not that anyone would come.

If *he* had been his father, he would've been here already. But Dad had never understood how much he loved this place. He'd never think of looking here. Assuming he'd bother to look anywhere. Mom might suggest it, but Dad would dismiss the idea with a "don't be ridiculous" and that would be the end of it.

What about the Tennisons? They'd be at their summer cabin, for sure. They might row over to the island and look around the cove. Would it be so bad if they found him? Maybe. Beth might be ticked off because he hadn't answered her letters. Then again, she wasn't the moody type; she wouldn't hold a grudge. She never had before. Anyway, he trusted her because of the danger game. Because of the oath.

But that was ages ago, the voice cut in. *And it was Diggon who swore that oath. Not you, cowering in a thicket of broom bushes. What would*

*Beth think of you now? And Field? The danger
game never meant to hurt anybody. Never meant
to kill.*

I didn't, I didn't . . .

But you let it happen.

He pressed his hands hard against the sides of
his head, trying to shut out the voice, trying to
press away the pain.

Chapter 11

While they were building the fire, Uncle Rob cruised around with his video camera. "Just ignore him," said Beth. She gave Chelsea an apologetic smile. "He does this all the time, recording the moment. Would you believe we have fifteen videos of Tidewater Beachfires? One for every year of my life. All of them totally boring."

"No way," Field laughed. "That time you got marshmallow stuck in your hair was cool. Remember how we had to use chewing gum to get it out?"

Beth chuckled. "Remember Mom's birthday, when Dad put a board on the table to make it bigger and we leaned on it just as she was blowing out the candles — "

"And the whole cake tipped into her lap! Remember that, Mom?"

"How could I forget? It's the highlight of

Tennison's Videothon. Don't worry, Chelsea. You won't leave here till you've suffered through it, along with the rest of us."

Suffered through it? Even though they groaned and complained, Chelsea could tell they enjoyed the videos, even looked forward to watching them. Another family tradition. Served with popcorn, no doubt.

Strange, that her dad was the professional photographer, yet how many family pictures did she have? Did Mom even have an album? She thought about the expensive cameras Dad had sent her, all of them unused, still tucked inside their cushiony packages. Sorry Dad, she had wanted to say. No natural disasters to photograph here. Unless you count Simon.

Uncle Rob put down the camera and handed Field his Swiss army knife. "You can sharpen the roasting sticks, but careful you don't cut off a finger. They aren't on the menu."

"*Dad!*" Beth rolled her eyes. "That's gross."

"But good on video," Field said. "All that blood."

"Some fire, eh, Chelsea?" Uncle Rob squatted beside her and stuck a wiener on the end of a stick. "Nothing like a good campfire."

Chelsea nodded and clasped her hands tightly to keep them from shaking. She felt the urge again, the urge to strike a match and set things blazing. It will pass, she repeated to herself.

"How do you like your marshmallows?" Beth asked.

Chelsea shrugged. "I've never had them like this before."

"What?" Everyone gaped. "Seriously? Quick, Dad, record the moment."

"Guess I've been deprived," she said.

They laughed, thinking she was kidding, and proceeded to argue about which way was best. Her aunt and uncle liked theirs toasted a light golden brown. Field waited until his marshmallow caught fire, then shook out the flames and gobbled down the whole black mess while skewering on another.

Not Beth. She turned her marshmallow carefully over the coals until there was the barest hint of a bubble. She pulled off that layer, popped it in her mouth, then roasted the gooey, melted centre. Once that layer was gone, the new centre was roasted. Layer after layer until only a gummy residue remained on the stick.

"Try it my way," Field said with a sticky grin. "It's way faster so you get to eat more."

But Chelsea preferred Beth's way. There was something satisfying about peeling off the layers, seeing how far you could go before there was nothing left. And the careful turning over the coals forced her hands to be steady.

Later, Aunt Carolyn started to sing.

Fire's burning, fire's burning
Draw nearer, draw nearer . . .

"Come on," she said. "Isn't anyone going to join me? I don't do solos."

"Sure," Uncle Rob said heartily. "We'll all join you. How about a round? Carolyn first, then me, then you kids."

Beth gave an exaggerated groan. "Why do we always have to do this? You guys turn everything into a Grade Two field trip."

"And who acts like a Grade Two-er half the time?" Field teased. "Fish-breath, that's who. Chelsea'll sing, won't you?"

"She better," Beth laughed. "You get a detention if you don't take part."

"That's right," said Uncle Rob. "It's the cooperative spirit around here."

Aunt Carolyn looked around the fire. "Is everybody ready? I'll start." She giggled as Beth and Field pulled faces. "Cut it out, you two. This is serious. The recorder's running."

"So's Beth's nose!" Field exclaimed, clowning for the camera. "Hurry up, you better catch it!"

Beth groaned. "Talk about Grade Two-ers. Chelsea, you're lucky you don't have a brother."

Finally, they started to sing.

Their voices rose and drifted far out over the water. When they finished one verse they started again because no one had decided when they should stop. At times Chelsea thought she heard another voice. A deeper voice that came from somewhere over her shoulder. But when she looked, there was only the water, black and smooth as satin.

After the tenth time, when Field rolled on the ground crying, "Help! Stop!" the voices wound down . . .

In the gloaming, in the gloaming
Come sing and be merry.

. . . and they listened to the echoes fade into the night.

It was Field who broke the silence. "What's a gloaming?"

The corners of Chelsea's mouth twitched in a smile.

It was a chilly night. Uncle Rob put another log on the fire and they moved in closer, watching the swirl of smoke and the flare-up of sparks. "You girls want to stay here for a while?" he asked. "The rest of us — yes, that means you, Field — are packing it in."

"Sure," said Beth. "That is, if you want to?" She turned to Chelsea.

Chelsea stared into the fire. "Sure."

"You've got till this log burns. Then douse the fire and come up. Got that? And Chelsea, don't go swimming after any more boats."

"He's packed up the camera so he can't record the moment," said Field.

"Give me a break." He cuffed Field playfully as they followed Aunt Carolyn along the beach. "See you in a bit, girls."

They listened as Field whined his way up to the cabin. "Why can't I stay? I'm ten. Beth got to stay up late when she was ten. It's not fair! *Mom!*" The door slammed shut and all was quiet.

"That was amazing what you did," Beth said after a while. "I mean, about the boat. Have you done stuff like that before? Like, rescued something? Or done something sort of scary and dangerous?"

Chelsea shrugged. She held a stick in the flames, wanting to do something with her hands, wanting to talk to Beth but not knowing what to say. She wished Field had stayed; he lightened things up. Beth seemed to expect something.

Why is it always like this? she thought, with a rush of anger. Everybody expects something. You give them what they want and they still want more. Wasn't it enough I rowed the boat? That's all I wanted. Not questions and answers. Not I'll-tell-you-if-you-tell-me confessions. She sensed that Beth wanted to relate to her in some way. But I can't, she felt like saying. Not now. It's too soon and too late and whatever I touch and whatever I feel it's —

"I've got something for you," Beth said suddenly, reaching into her pocket. "It's kind of squashed, but . . . I'm lousy at art. It's supposed to be a crane. Here, if you pull the sides out a bit . . ."

"Wings." Chelsea sighed, remembering a grey November day coloured by origami.

"There's this legend or something," Beth continued. "If you make a thousand cranes for someone who's sick . . . Well, I don't know if it works, but here's the first one. For your dad." She smiled. "Just 999 left to go."

Chelsea looked at the limp crane resting in the palm of her hand. Beth had obviously cut a square from the comic section to make it, and judging by the network of lines, had folded and refolded many times until she got it right. Or as close to right as she could get. In the firelight Chelsea could see where the ink had smudged, running the colours, probably from sweaty fingers. It was a battered, bedraggled crane, no doubt about it. Still . . .

"Beth," she began, turning to her cousin. "I — " She looked away, disturbed by the strange course her feelings were taking. "Never mind." She swallowed them down, whatever words she meant to say. Swallowed them hard, so they wouldn't rise up again. Cupping the crane in her hands as if it were a living thing, she watched the fire die down.

Chapter 12

He needed to move. Needed to get outside himself for a while.

He unlocked the shed and took out the oars. Then he turned the boat over and pushed it down the bank, onto the beach, and into the water.

The moon shone hazily through scraps of cloud. Stars appeared, then disappeared. Each pull of the oar fired the water with phosphorescence. It was so quiet, for a moment he felt something close to comfort.

He rowed past the island, out of the cove, and into the basin.

A fire flickered on the far shore, at Tidewater. He felt a sudden ache, remembering other fires on that beach. Remembering Beth.

The light drew him closer, but not too close. Hidden by the darkness, he pulled in the oars and gazed at the figures around the fire. Beth's dad, zooming around with his video camera, as usual.

Her mom, trying to juggle marshmallows. Field, drawing figure eights in the air with a flaming stick. Beth, putting another log on the fire. All of them teasing, joking, laughing.

All except that other person, sitting still as a wooden carving. Who was she? Her profile, even from a distance, looked solemn and mysterious. Exotic almost, as if she had floated in on the tide from some faraway place.

Don't be stupid, he told himself. She's probably one of Beth's friends from school, giggly and unbearable. It never worked, bringing school friends here. He'd done it a few times, but it was always a disaster. They didn't know the rituals. They didn't belong.

The sound of singing drifted across the water. Beth's mom always started the singing, he remembered. Beth always grumbled but eventually joined in. He recognized the round, *Fire's burning, fire's burning*, the separate parts weaving in and around and through, becoming a rich, multilayered whole. Something welled up inside, a hurt so big he felt an embarrassing urge to cry.

Draw nearer, draw nearer . . .

He wanted to. It would be so easy to row into shore and join the group around the fire. He knew they would welcome him. Beth's dad would say something predictable like, "What a surprise," and her mom would force all the leftovers on him. Field would hand him a roasting stick, barely missing his eye probably, in his usual hyper way. And Beth — he wasn't sure about Beth. But they would draw him in, closer and closer, and make it easy for him to pretend nothing had changed.

But everything had changed. Lowering the oars quietly, he turned the boat and rowed away. Before long, even the voices were silent.

Dad hadn't liked him singing. "What? You're in the choir?" He shook his head, disgusted.

Tough, Diggon thought. He liked to sing, so he'd sing. He liked digging holes in the ground, too. So what? So what if he hated contact sports. So what if his own father thought he was a wimp. "Come on, you'll love rugby. I was team captain when I was your age."

Bully for you, Dad.

Before rugby, he'd been signed up and outfitted for ice hockey and soccer, both of which he detested. But no matter how hard he tried, it wasn't good enough. "Not like that!" Dad yelled. "You'll never be good at anything."

Swimming, Dad. Have you seen me swim to the island and back? How about diving? Rowing, too — have you noticed?

Stupid question. Him, notice something *I'm* interested in? Not likely.

They both enjoyed fishing, but Diggon always managed to screw things up, get the lines tangled, get a hook in his finger, let the fish get away. "What are you?" Dad shouted. "A frigging vegetarian or something?"

Dad did give him credit for one thing. Perseverance. His ability to keep at it, doggedly searching until he found a solution, whether it was a computer problem or a broken outboard motor. Like the time they were stranded in the strait, when Diggon tinkered with the motor until he got it going again. Dad slapped him on the back, he was so pleased. The motor — and Diggon — hummed all the way home.

He hadn't slapped him on the back when Diggon found the arrowhead. "It's just a rock. Why don't you do something useful instead of wasting time digging around the beach? Arrowhead, pah!"

Diggon persevered. He took the arrowhead to the archaeologist at the Royal B.C. Museum and had it verified. "See?" He proudly showed Dad the note. "It's even signed by the archaeologist. It *is* an arrowhead, made from basalt. The whole basin is full of Native artifacts, he said. You know the boatworks on the other side? That site is 3000 years old, he said. Imagine, Dad!"

"So what's it worth?"

And just like that the joy of discovery drained away, his father's words more stinging than a slap in the face.

So what's Dad going to think about the other night?

I don't know.

But the horrifying thought came to him that Dad might be pleased in some perverted way. Those kids were what he wanted Diggon to be. One of the gang. Hard. Tough. Not a kid who sang rounds. Not a kid who cried in the dark.

Once his English class had to write an essay on who they most admired. Diggon deliberately misunderstood the directions and wrote about the man he least admired, his dad. Dad the heavyweight, heavy with sarcasm. Dad the jock, playing old-timers' hockey, drinking beer with the guys after every practice, reliving the days when their teams rah-rah-rahed their way through high school and university. Dad the hunk, touching up the grey hairs, showing off his biceps and triceps, his hard, flat belly — "Come on, Diggon, give us a punch. Not like that, harder, for crissake." Dad the money-maker. "Tennison? He's just a teacher. I make three times what he makes." As if anybody cared.

Who did Diggon most admire? The soft-spoken archaeologist, digging into the past.

Why, then, had he let himself get suckered so brutally into the present?

He hated the move to Vancouver. In Vancouver he was out of his element, a stranger. But he knew that if you didn't flail around and draw attention to yourself, you were all right. He knew how to act invisible, how to drift through the days and weeks and months, without really paying attention to anything. Just getting through.

He was surprised when Blake and the others came up to him that day at the mall and asked him to the party. He had worn his invisibility for so long he had begun to accept it as his usual way of being. So he was surprised and — he had to admit — pleased. He discovered there was a coolness about him that did attract attention.

He had a great time at the party.

Until it was over.

Chapter 13

Chelsea and Beth were up early, making cranes. The table on the verandah was covered with squares of all sizes, cut from every kind of paper available. "It won't matter, will it?" Beth wondered. "I mean, if we don't have that special paper."

"I don't think so," said Chelsea. She had cut squares from a Canadian Living magazine and was deftly folding chocolate pecan cheesecakes and strawberry meringue tortes. "These are delicious cranes. If the gods do grant wishes, I think they'll like these ones even better."

"Good point. Make do with what you have, that's what Dad the philosopher always says. Speaking of which . . . "

"Morning, girls. That's quite a flock you've got there. Mind if I record the moment?"

"Do we have a choice?" Beth grinned into the camera.

"What're you planning to do with all these cranes?"

"Good question, Dad. I'll turn that over to my cousin, the origami expert." She gave Chelsea a nudge. "You're on."

Chelsea glanced up shyly. "I'd like to hang them like mobiles. Maybe right here, on the verandah. Hundreds and hundreds of them."

"Brilliant!" Beth exclaimed. "I'll get some twigs and some thread."

She found a needle and helped Chelsea string the finished cranes together. Then they attached them to crossed twigs and hung them from the rafters. Even Field joined in. "I'm cutting up this old sports magazine, see? So my cranes will be made from hockey players. Cool, eh?"

"Totally," said Beth. "Especially since they're on ice."

"Can we make some room for breakfast?" Mom brought out a pitcher of orange juice and a plate of toast. "Beth, how about setting the table?"

Sunshine flooded the verandah and lit the multicoloured cranes. A light breeze rustled through their wings.

"Good thing they're not real." Field pushed his cranes aside and began buttering toast.

"Why's that?"

"Because they're flying right over the table where we're eating. Bird droppings, get it?"

Beth looked at Chelsea and groaned. "Back to Grade Two."

"What's on the agenda today?" Mom asked, pouring more orange juice. "Let's get things organized."

"We're making cranes all morning," said Beth. "After lunch we're rowing to the island."

"And I'm taking my casting rod," said Field.

"No way. You're not even invited."

"Don't worry, I'll tie up the boat and I won't bug you. Much. I want to do some fishing. I can go, can't I, Dad?"

"Whatever you decide is fine with me. You kids work it out. I'm into some heavy relaxing."

"Me too," said Mom. "But I wouldn't mind a fish for supper."

"See? Told you I could go." Field gave his sister a smug look.

"Let's get this table cleared, if everybody's finished breakfast," said Dad. "Another hundred cranes before lunch, is that the plan?"

"Two hundred, easy," said Beth. "Maybe even three. You want to help? Chelsea's good at it. She'll show you how."

Chelsea handed him a square of the classified ads and started the instructions. "Side to side, corner to corner . . . "

"Not bad, once you get the hang of it," he said, examining his finished crane. "Reminds me of your dad when he was a kid. He was always making things with his hands. Used to fold pirate hats out of newspaper. But once he got his camera, all he ever wanted to do was take pictures."

"How come you and Uncle Mark never see each other? Or even write?" Beth asked bluntly. "You're *brothers*. Did you have a fight or something?"

Her father started folding a glossy chicken casserole. "No, nothing like that. I don't know, really. He's six years younger than me. We were never very close. Just went our separate ways, I guess. Grew apart." He shrugged. "Things happen. It doesn't mean we don't like each other, we're just different. We hardly even know each other anymore."

"Now we know Chelsea, right?" Beth grinned at her cousin. "And we're not that different."

"Yeah," said Field. "You're both bird-brains."

Chelsea tossed him another square of paper and smiled.

Chapter 14

From his hiding place in the broom bushes, Diggon watched the three get out of the boat and make their way up the path to the wooded area. Beth and Field rushed about as usual, their eyes darting in a hundred directions, afraid they might miss something.

He remembered how ticked Beth had been when he found the arrowhead. "Why you?" she had fumed. "I've been looking my whole life for one of those things."

"Me too! And I found this when I wasn't even looking."

"Oh sure, rub it in."

"I bent down to pick up the oar and there it was, right at my feet."

When was that, three years ago? Four?

He turned his attention back to the island. Beth was in a great mood, leaping about, acting like a tour guide. A few words carried across the water, but even without hearing them he could pretty well guess what she was saying. "Up there's the eagle's nest, here's where we camp sometimes, over there's Heron Cove and the dock and the beach, a good clam-digging beach where arrowheads are sometimes, but hardly ever, found. On the hill above the beach is the Spence place where — " Will she mention me? he wondered. Yeah, knowing girls. She'll probably tell her about those dumb letters I wrote, too.

Whenever Beth paused for breath Field took over the role of tour guide. "See that tree? That's where a guy hanged himself, that's why it's called Deadman's Island . . . ."

Funny how the two of them seemed to be competing for the new girl's attention.

Who was she? He peered through the broom and tried to focus on her. What was she doing with Beth? He couldn't imagine two girls more unalike. She was taller than Beth, long-legged and slender. Even with her oversize shirt he could tell she was more developed, whereas Beth was still built like a ten-year-old. And where Beth clambered, this girl moved like a dancer, with —

He paused, searching for a word. "Grace." The word startled him. Where had he picked that up? But having said it, he knew it was right. She moved with grace, almost floated up the path. As Beth and Field jabbered on, she listened, nodded, turned her head, tossed back her hair, all with grace. She probably speaks with grace too, he thought. If that's possible.

And that hair, hovering around her face like a cloud, swirling over her shoulders and down to her waist like a black cape glinting with reddish-gold threads. A person could hide in hair like that, he thought.

Maybe that was the idea.

So who is she? Diggon wondered, as the three left his field of vision and moved to the far side of the island. A new neighbour? A friend from school? A sister Beth never knew she had, given up for adoption at birth and —

Nobody, as far as you're concerned. The voice hammered into his thoughts. *She's off-limits to the likes of you. And who are you to talk of grace?*

He looked down at the yellow petals he was shredding, the pile of stiff green stems he had crushed. The muscles of his face tensed and his eyes became moist. He turned his back on the island and crawled deeper into the tunnel. When he reached the end he clamped his hands over his ears, shutting out the distant sounds of laughter. But he couldn't shut out the sounds of the seed pods snapping in the afternoon heat, a dry sound, like the soft cracking of bones.

Chapter 15

"Any bites yet?"

Field turned from his casting spot on the rock and gave his sister a withering glare. "I just started."

Beth and Chelsea chewed on long pieces of grass and watched as he reeled in the line, checked his lure, drew back his arm, and cast again, glancing over his shoulder to see if they'd noticed his fine casting form.

They had. "Good one!" Beth clapped. "Any bites yet?" She laughed, then turned to Chelsea and said quietly, "You're sure you want to?"

Chelsea nodded.

"It's not as if he doesn't deserve it, right? I mean, after yesterday and the boat and everything."

"Yes!" Chelsea's eyes glinted with mischief. "You don't have to keep justifying it."

"OK. I mean, it's not as if — "

Chelsea gave an exasperated sigh.

"OK, OK. When I give the word."

"What's the word?"

"Now!"

They grabbed their packs, ran across the island, leaped into the boat, and pushed it away from shore. "Any minute now," Beth said, picking up the oars. "Any minute — "

"Hey!" The shout came from the far side of the island.

"What did I tell you?" Beth laughed.

"I'll get you for this!" Field ran down the path, fumbling with his rod and tackle box. "Bring that boat back! You zit-head!"

"Sor-ree!" Beth taunted. "It wasn't tied up!" Shaking with laughter, she rowed as hard as she could, away from the island and out of the cove.

"You expect me to swim for it, or what?" Field yelled. "Come back! Chelsea, make her come back!" He picked up a rock and hurled it after them. "You — !" he swore. "You're dead, Beth! I know it was your idea. You're dead!"

He kept throwing rocks and shouting curses until the boat was out of sight. Finally, hot with anger and frustration he took his rod and tackle back to the casting rock. Might as well do something, he figured. Might even catch something. Sooner or later they'd be back. Then he'd get even with his sister. In a big way.

"What do you think, Chelsea? How long should we leave him?"

They had rowed back to Tidewater, pulled up the boat, and were now sitting on the beach. "I don't know." Chelsea stretched out her legs and leaned back on her elbows. "He's your brother."

"Three or four days?"

"Till he's well done?"

"Or just moderately stewed?"

"I think he'll be totally stewed."

"Right." Beth gave a malicious chuckle. "Speaking of stewed, I'm boiling." She stripped off her shorts and T-shirt and rummaged in her pack for the sunscreen. "Aren't you boiling in that thing?" she wondered, eyeing Chelsea's shirt. "You should wear your swimsuit underneath, like me."

"I don't want to get burned."

"Why don't you use sunscreen? I've got lots, if you want."

"Might as well." Chelsea squirted some lotion into her hand and smoothed it over her legs. "Maybe we should go back for him."

"Nah. Let him simmer a bit longer. He deserves it." Beth slathered more sunscreen over her arms and shoulders. "Actually, he's not so bad, for a brother. But he's better here than at home. At home in Victoria, I mean. It's like we've got a summertime truce."

"Until today."

"He'll be OK. Anyway, it's two against one."

"I used to wish I had a brother," Chelsea said. "Or a sister. Then I wished I had a dad." And a mom, she added silently.

"Yeah," Beth sighed. For a while neither spoke. "Have you ever . . . " she began tentatively. "I mean, have you ever had, like, a boyfriend?"

"Have you?" Chelsea rolled onto her side, facing her cousin.

Beth felt her face grow hot. "Well, actually, I have. Sort of."

"How can you have a sort of a boyfriend?"

"OK. I'll tell you. But only because you're my cousin. There's this guy, right? And one night we were — "

"Hey, Beth! Hey, you guys!"

Startled, they looked up at the sound of the voice and saw Field running across the beach, waving his arms and yelling, "Guess what!"

"Didn't we leave him on the island?" said Chelsea.

"Yeah!" Beth scratched her head, bewildered. "How did he get back? It's too far to swim, at least for — "

"Beth!" he cried. He bent over double to catch his breath. "You'll never guess, you'll just — "

"Calm down, would you. How did you get here?"

"Diggon!" His face split in a wide grin. "He's back! He's back for the danger game!"

PART 5

THE DANGER GAME

Chapter 16

It started three years ago, on a hot, listless day. Not a breath of wind, not a scrap of cloud. Beth sat on the dock in Heron Cove and dangled her legs in the water, while Diggon and Field argued about what to do next.

"Let's row to the island."

"Done it already."

"Catch bullheads."

"Boring."

Beth watched a school of tiny fish swim by her feet, tickling her toes. "Why don't we hike along the old railway line? And swim in the lake."

"Too far."

"Too hot."

Then Diggon made a suggestion. "How about the bay? Out in the strait."

Beth stopped splashing her feet and looked at him, surprised. They'd never considered going to the strait before. Not on their own.

"It'll be way cooler out there," he went on. "We can take the runabout, with the outboard. Dad just filled it with gas."

Field gave Beth a worried look. "We're not allowed, are we?"

"Come on!" Diggon grinned. "Who's going to know?"

Beth picked up the hoochie-koochie lying on the dock and twirled it, making the shiny pink strips spin out in a circle. Sunlight caught the tinsel, flashing twists of silver. That's what this day needs, she decided. A flash of silver. A lure. She turned to Diggon. "You're right. Who's going to know?"

They moved closer, heads together, working out a plan. "I'll tell Mom we're going across the basin to Madison Cove," Diggon said. "She's so busy canning salmon she won't even know I've gone."

"What about your dad?" Field asked.

"He's in town working, what else?"

"Can we go home first and get a snack? I'm starving."

Beth rolled her eyes. "Don't you ever think of anything else?"

"Takes too long," Diggon said. "I'll get something."

After he'd gone, Field turned to Beth. "Will we get back in time? Mom said — "

"Look, if you're worried, stay here. Or row

home by yourself and tell Mom I'll be back later, with Diggon. Actually, maybe you are too young. Maybe you better — "

"No way. I'm coming. I wasn't worried anyway, just wondering."

"And you swear you won't tell?" Beth held the hook of the hoochie-koochie over his arm.

Field pushed it away. "Yes, I swear!"

Diggon returned with a bag of chips and cans of pop. "This'll be great! A real adventure."

"Have you been there before?" Beth asked as they put on their life jackets and climbed into the boat. "Without your dad, I mean."

Diggon untied the rope, pushed the boat away from the dock, and pulled the cord of the outboard motor. "Nope," he said, speaking above the roar. "This'll be the first time." Once they were out of the cove he increased the speed. Soon they were skimming through the harbour, towards Whiffen Spit.

Beth clung to the seat as the boat bounced over the water. Her face glistened with spray, her eyes prickled with salt, her body shook with the vibrations of the boat. She could feel the pull of the tide as Diggon guided the boat around the spit, through what Dad called the danger zone. Here, you had to move slowly and cautiously. The passage was so narrow you had to be careful not to get swept into the shallows. You also had to watch out for kelp beds, otherwise the prop could get tangled in the long, streaming blades of kelp. "That's why I don't want you kids out of the basin," Dad always said. "Too many danger zones, even on a calm day. And when the wind picks up, or if it gets foggy — which it can do at the drop of a hat — it's even worse. So you can stop nagging. Unless I'm with you, you're not to leave the basin. Got it?"

But today the temptation was too delicious. Everything had an edge. Everything felt sunstruck and sharp. Beth hugged her knees and smiled, exhilarated by the speed and the sense of adventure. Diggon caught her eye and smiled back.

Once they were safely around the spit, they sped into the strait and along the shoreline until they reached the bay.

"We should call it Watermelon Bay," said Field, "like in the song, you know?" In an off-key voice he began to sing.

> *Down by the Bay, where the watermelons grow*
> *Back to my home, I dare not go.*
> *'Cause if I do, my mother will say,*
> *Did you ever see a whale with a hoochie-koochie tail?*
> *Down by the Bay.*

"Mom's going to say more than that if she ever finds out," said Beth. "So make sure you keep quiet about it."

"I saw this place on a map," Diggon said. "It's

really called Mystic Bay."

"Why?" Field wondered.

"Because it's mystical and mysterious," said Beth. "Or maybe it's because you see things differently here, like in the song."

The boat crunched onto the shingle beach as Diggon cut the motor and tipped the outboard. They climbed out and tied the boat to a log while Diggon opened the bag of chips. "Let's say we're never going to tell anyone else what we see or do here."

Field gave him a worried look. "What *are* we going to do here?"

"Things we don't do anywhere else," said Diggon.

"Dangerous things," said Beth. "Not *really* dangerous, just fun dangerous."

Diggon grinned. "Exciting dangerous. Close to real danger without going over the edge."

"You know how Dad always talks about the danger zone? By the spit where the tide's really strong?"

"Yeah . . . So?"

"So we've passed the danger zone and now we're in the game zone. The danger game, get it?" Beth warmed to the subject. "And whenever we come here, one of us has to invent a danger game to play."

"Yeah, but — "

"Look, Field. You're lucky we even let you

come, isn't he, Diggon?"

"No kidding. You're not scared, are you?"

Field glanced from one to the other. How dangerous could it get? Beth wasn't stupid, neither was Diggon, although he'd never admit it to them. "No, I'm not scared."

"Good!" Diggon slapped him on the back. "First, we'll explore and check things out. Then we can decide on today's game."

"Who picks first?"

"Me," said Beth. "I thought of it. But first we have to swear an oath."

"All right!" Field exclaimed. "They always do that in books."

"Well this time we're doing it for real. We'll swear an oath of secrecy and prick our fingers to seal it."

"Like blood brothers, you mean?"

"Right." Diggon took out his knife and opened the blade. "What's the oath going to be?"

"It has to have special words," Beth said. "Since it's Mystic Bay."

"Watermelon Bay," said Field.

"No, Mystic Bay sounds better. But your song can be like the anthem, when we're here. As long as you don't overdo it. Now, about the oath . . . "

Diggon picked up a piece of wood and began whittling, while the others finished the chips and tried to think of an appropriate oath.

"Why don't we just promise something and

then say a swear?" Field grinned. "I know lots of swears."

Beth flashed him a look. "If you're not going to take this seriously, forget it."

"All right, all right."

"I've got the words now," she said. "You guys ready? Repeat after me." She cleared her throat and assumed a solemn air. "We promise to keep Mystic Bay a secret. No matter how differently we see things. We promise to play the danger game and keep each other safe from getting hurt. No, safe from harm. That sounds better."

"Now we prick fingers," said Diggon, holding out his knife.

One by one they pricked their baby fingers. "There!" Beth said, smiling. The moment felt huge with significance. "Now you can swear."

They did.

"One more thing," said Diggon. "Let's say everyone has to agree on the danger game before we can play it. No one is forced to do anything. Agreed?"

"Agreed."

Mystic Bay was perfectly sheltered, hemmed in by rocky headlands. A steep, rugged island filled the entrance. The only way into the bay was through a narrow passage on either side of the island. From the strait the bay was nearly invisible, so they could pull the boat onto the beach without anyone knowing it was there.

A point jutted out on one side of the beach, accessible only at low tide. It was heavily wooded, with overhanging branches perfect for rope swings. On the other side of the beach was a creek, rippling down a gully from the woods to the sea. Behind the beach was a grassy hill, perfect for sliding down. Beyond the hill was the forest.

From the first summer to the last, the summer Diggon moved away, they developed a whole litany of games.

Crawling through stinging nettles without getting stung.

Sliding down the hill on windbreakers, and when that got too tame, setting out obstacles — coiled ropes of kelp or large chunks of driftwood.

Snapping whips of kelp and trusting the others not to hit your feet, or wrapping one person mummy-style in coils of slimy kelp, then racing off to hide while the mummy got unwound.

Playing squirt-tag with sea sacs, the seaweed that looked like clumps of stubby green fingers.

Creeping along the muddy creek bed, looking for tracks and finding them. Deer, raccoon, once a cougar.

Jumping into the water at the same time, seeing who could hold their breath the longest.

Plunging from the rope swing into the water, making sure they cleared the jagged rocks before letting go.

Crossing the gully by walking over a fallen tree, slippery with moss. Branches jutted out every few steps, good for hanging onto, but tricky to get past. Walking across the windfall was Field's game. Beth added the blindfolds.

One day, scrabbling down a rocky slope to explore a smaller bay, Field spotted a wasp nest. "Stop!" He held out a hand to keep the others back. "I'm going round the long way. I hate those things."

"Don't be a chicken," said Diggon. "They only attack if you disturb them."

"Easy for you to talk," Beth said. "Field swells up like a watermelon if he gets stung."

"Really? Nothing like that happens to me. But you know what? Even if you disturb them, if you stand perfectly still they'll just buzz around you and won't sting."

"Oh, sure." Beth wasn't convinced.

"No kidding, I've done it. It freaks you out, standing there, but as long as you don't panic and run, they honestly don't sting. They think you're a tree or something. If you run and yell and wave your arms, they think you're attacking. Then they go wild."

"I dare you to try it." Beth spoke without thinking. As soon as the words were out, she realized her mistake.

Diggon grinned. "Is that your game for today?"

"No, I didn't say that. I meant — "

"Great! Let's make this a danger game. OK, Field?"

"You don't have to agree," Beth said quickly. "You can pass if you want."

"Yeah, but — " Field took a deep breath, trying not to look at the wasps flying in and out of the nest. "OK," he said reluctantly. "I agree."

"Are you sure? You can change your mind."

"I said OK."

Diggon turned to Beth. "What about you?"

She glanced at Field, annoyed. Why did he have to agree? It would have been an easy out, if he'd simply said "pass." Now it was up to her. The rules were clear. Everyone had to agree, otherwise they wouldn't do it. But if you were the one who backed out, the others could give you a bad time. Especially if you were the only girl. She'd already spoiled one day by saying "pass." Too much of that and she'd risk spoiling the danger game completely. Or give them an excuse to leave her out altogether. "Oh, all right," she said. "What do we do?"

"We stand beside the nest," Diggon said. "I'll throw a rock at it. When the wasps come out, freeze. No matter what happens, don't move."

Beth swallowed hard, took one look at her brother's white face, and quickly looked away.

"Trust me," said Diggon. "It works. As long as you stand still. OK?" He picked up a rock and threw it. "Freeze!" he yelled.

The wasps swarmed out. Beth gasped in horror. How could there be so many! She forced herself to look straight ahead, feeling them buzzing around her head, face, arms, legs, ankles. Oh God, in her hair, one by her mouth. She felt the tickling of sticky feet on her cheek, on the inside of her arm. I can't stand this, she screamed silently, I can't . . . She forced herself not to break away in a panic, forced herself not to breathe because if she did she'd scream them into attacking her.

She could see Field out of the corner of her eye. His face was taut with fear, his eyes glazed. There were no wasps around his head or shoulders, none on his arms. She glanced down and saw one wasp creeping on his leg beneath the edge of his shorts. If it crawled inside, got trapped under the fabric . . .

But it didn't. Within seconds, it flew away. Within seconds — minutes? hours? — they had all flown away.

They ran then, breaking the freeze at the same time.

"It really worked, Diggon! You were right! Not a single sting!"

"See, I told you! How many did you have on you? Man, I thought I'd die when I felt them on my neck. And I thought one was going to crawl up my nose!"

"Yeah? Well I felt this one in my hair . . . "

They tried to outdo each other with wasp stories, while Beth collapsed on the beach, gripping the backs of her arms to control the shaking. "That's it, you guys," she said, breathing hard. "That's the last danger game I'm playing."

"And was it?" Chelsea whispered from the top bunk.

"No way," said Beth.

This was the first night Chelsea hadn't gone right to sleep. After climbing up the ladder and tucking herself under the down quilt, she had asked Beth about the danger game Field was so fired up about. From the bottom bunk, Beth told her.

"We got to know every inch of that bay, the beach and the creek and the woods, everything," she said. "Those were the best times." The three of them sharing the secret, speeding out of the safety ring of the basin, through the danger zone, into the forbidden territory of Mystic Bay.

"And your parents never found out?" Chelsea asked. "They seem so watchful."

"Yeah, well. It's not like we went there every day. Only once in a while, when the weather was perfect. And we never stayed that long. Diggon's mom always thought he was at our place or across the basin. His dad was always in town, working. My mom was at the university most of the time, working on her Master's. Dad likes vegging around and reading so he's always happy when we row to the cove and fool around over there. And he trusts us to be safe," she added guiltily.

"You said that you passed once?"

"Yeah, it was getting windy in the basin and I knew it would be even rougher on the strait. So I made Diggon turn back. We never did anything *that* dangerous, really. Field's probably the only one who'd want to play again."

"Oh, I don't know," said Chelsea. "I'd like to see the bay."

"Seriously?"

"Why not? I know all about it, now. You broke your oath, you know, telling me."

"I guess lightning will strike any minute," Beth said with a laugh. "It's over now, anyway. It was just a kid's game."

"But you loved it."

"Yeah. I loved it."

"So what's this Diggon like?"

Beth smiled in the dark. "Nothing special," she said. "It's been a long time." At least that part was true. She rolled onto her side, hugging the pillow to her chest, hugging the words, *He's back*.

Chelsea lay awake, struggling to control her breathing, the pounding in her chest, the suffocating feel of the nightmare. She concentrated on sounds, the rampage of tree frogs, the *whoooooo . . . who* of an owl that faded away on a low warble, quivering in the still night. Quiet, quiet sounds.

She wished she could hear the sea.

In Hawaii, even though Dad's house was on the hillside, she could hear the surf. From outside, from inside, from every room in the house. Day and night, hour after hour, the breakers rolled in and rolled over, pounding, crashing, rolling in and over again. Minute after minute, the one thing she could always count on.

Here, the sea flowed with the tide, in and out, but softly.

She wished she could feel calm. Wished she could stop the itching in her fingers, the urge to —

No.

She wouldn't give in again.

She heard a creak in the lower bunk, the rustle of covers as Beth turned over, sighing in her sleep. Quietly, she pushed back the quilt and crept down the ladder. She put on her bathrobe and turned the door handle. Her bare feet padded softly across the floor.

She heard a coughing sound and froze.

Then carried on, through the doorway, across the verandah, down the steps, and onto the lawn. A heavy dew silvered the grass. She ran quickly towards the meadow, her white bathrobe flowing behind.

The meadow shone with moonlight. Spider webs glistened. Driftwood glistened. She ran down the path, over the wooden bridge and onto the beach, her feet tingling against the cold stones.

A fire, she thought. A fire to warm her feet.

Her fingers curled around a small box. Strange. How did that get there? She didn't remember putting the matchbox in her bathrobe pocket, but how fortunate. Now she could light a fire.

No. She pulled out her hand and filled it with stones, picking up flat ones to skip across the water. One, two, three . . . Could she make a stone skip seven times? Eight? Maybe. It was hard to count in the darkness.

The tide was so high the water lapped the scorched remains of last night's fire. That's what she needed, a fire to warm things up.

No! Again she forced her hand from her pocket and clasped it tightly. What's the matter with you? she cried silently. There's no danger, nothing can hurt you here, and it's just for a little while, isn't it? Dad will be off the critical list soon, won't he? He'll remember things and be able to walk again, won't he?

She forced herself away from the fire circle and stepped gingerly along the shore, feeling the broken shells and barnacles sharp against the soles of her feet. What about tomorrow? she wondered. And this other person, this Diggon. What would he be like? Another person to wonder and question, another person whose eyes might see inside . . .

Without thinking, she shook out a match, knelt down, and struck it against the side of a rock.

She held the flame in front of her face. Blue-violet, flaring to gold. Bright gold in the moonlight, bright against the silvery black sea. She waved her hand over it and through it. What about tomorrow? It didn't matter, now.

"Chelsea?"

"Ahhh!" She turned, startled. "Aunt Carolyn, I — "

"Are you all right?"

"Yes! I — " She tossed the burning match into the water. With a hiss and sputter it was gone. "I couldn't sleep," she said lamely.

"Neither could I." Aunt Carolyn sat on a log and tucked her robe around her legs. "A full moon does it to me every time. Here," she said, patting the log. "Have a seat."

Reluctantly, Chelsea sat beside her. What now? she wondered. Had her aunt seen her light the match? Would she start asking questions? She started to get up. "I really should — "

"No, no. Stay a while. Keep me company. I thought you were a ghost!" she laughed. "I was standing on the verandah and saw this misty white shape floating along the beach. Gave me quite an eerie feeling. But once my eyes woke up, I could make out your hair. And figured, that's got to be Chelsea."

"You're not disappointed? That I'm not a ghost?"

"Oh, I don't know," she teased. "Maybe just a

tad. Really, I'm glad you're here. It's about time we got to know the rest of the Tennison family."

Chelsea thought about this. "Did you — " she began hesitantly, "Did you know my dad?"

"No, I never met him. He was in England when Rob and I got married, and after that he was all over the place. But I'm looking forward to meeting him. Soon, I hope."

"Do you think . . . "

"Yes! Absolutely, positively, yes. Rob told me about his other accidents, how he bounces back in no time. But how about you?" She turned to Chelsea. "Are you settling in OK? Is there anything you — "

"I'm fine." Chelsea stiffened. Now it starts. Questions, questions . . .

But her aunt remained silent. They sat side by side, listening to the water lap the shore. When they both started to shiver and decided it was time to go in, Aunt Carolyn said, "If there is anything, anything at all you want to tell me — "

"I'm fine."

" — if you need someone to listen, I'm here."

Chelsea tightened her fingers around the matchbox. Inside her head, she chanted I'm fine, I'm fine and nothing's getting unfolded this time. I'm not making the same mistake, not this time. And I'm not going to tell. Not you, Aunt Carolyn, not anyone, never again.

Chapter 17

"Come on, Chelsea." Beth stuffed her backpack with cookies, apples, and grapes, slung it over her shoulder, and headed for the door. "Field! Aren't you ready yet?"

"Yeah, yeah." He finished arranging the lures in his tackle box and closed the lid.

"Come on, then."

"Beth, you've hardly touched your lunch. What's the big rush?" Mom asked. "You'd think you had a plane to catch."

"You're going fishing again?" said Dad. "Thought you were making more cranes."

"We've been making them all morning and our fingers are cramped. Right, Chelsea? Field, hurry up!"

"Can we take some chips?" he asked, putting a bag in his pack.

"You might as well," Mom muttered.

"Hope you have better luck this time," said

Dad. "Maybe tomorrow we'll take the cruiser out to the strait. Give Chelsea a tour. Good run of coho, from what I hear. Salmon are jumping into the boats."

"Sure, Dad."

"Have you all got sweaters and windbreakers? It can get cold in the basin if —"

"Mom! We're not going to the Arctic!"

Dad scowled. "No need to be snippy."

"Sorry. Are you ready, Field? Come on!"

"See you later," said Field.

"Not too much later," Mom called after them. "Could be a change in the weather."

"Not a chance," Dad said. "Clear as a bell out there."

"My turn to row," Field said as they pushed the boat into the water.

"Go ahead." Beth climbed into the bow. She was too excited to hold the oars let alone row the boat. Diggon was back!

What would he be like? And how would she look to him, after almost a year? At least her skin was clear, only three tiny zits when she checked this morning. Would he notice? She wished her hair was long enough to braid or something. She should never have had it cut. She wished she'd worn her black T-shirt instead of the turquoise one. No, this one made her tan look better. Would he notice? Would he care? She wished she could stop trembling. Wished she could be totally cool, like Chelsea. Wished her face would stop burning.

It was a wonder no one had said anything. Mom and Dad were usually so quick to notice the slightest little thing, especially with her. "How did you know?" she had often asked. "I don't get it!"

"Beth," they would say, "we can read you like a book."

Well, they hadn't noticed anything this morning. Maybe she was learning to hide things better. Too bad she hadn't learned sooner, during the letter business.

Oh no, she thought with alarm. What if he says something about my letters? She tried to remember what she'd written. Had she really signed them with X's and O's? Yes. Oh God, yes, she had.

It would've been bad enough facing him on her own, but now, with Field and Chelsea. . . But maybe it'll be better this way. Yes, she decided. The others will be a distraction. He won't notice me so much.

Oh God. She felt a sharp twisting inside, as an unspeakable thought came into her mind. What if he doesn't notice me at all?

Face it, Beth. There could be someone else. He could be totally different. His face could be a minefield of zits for all you know. Maybe he's shaved his head. Maybe he's got an earring in his nose. Or in his eyebrow. Maybe that's why he stopped writing, he's —

There he was. Waiting at the dock with the runabout, outboard attached, ready to go, raising his hand in a wave.

The sight of him made her weak. One minute her heart was in the right place, the next it had dropped into her toes. She felt a shiver in her spine, a tingling behind her knees, a queasy feeling in her stomach. How was it possible to feel so excited, so happy, and so sick all at the same time?

He was just as she remembered, only better. His brown hair was longer. He wasn't so skinny. More serious-looking than before, but cool and confident. Lean, muscled, tanned. Totally perfect.

Well, she could be cool and confident, too. She pictured herself getting out of the boat gracefully, saying, Hi, Diggon, how are you?, giving him a warm, meaningful smile. He'd smile back, his dark blue eyes shining, understanding her meaning. Then he'd brush against her, rest his hand lightly on her shoulder . . .

"Toss me the rope, Beth," he said as Field rowed in closer. "I'll pull you in."

"I can do it." The words took her by surprise. What was she doing? She hadn't meant to say that. She jumped out too fast, too eager, stumbled over an oar and fell hard on her knees. "Ow!" she cried.

Field howled with laughter. "Have a nice trip?"

"Are you OK?" Chelsea asked, concerned.

Beth got up, embarrassed beyond belief. She blushed, furious with herself, and snatched the rope from Diggon's hand. "I said I can do it. Why don't you move those oars before someone else has a nice trip?"

With fumbling fingers she tied up the rowboat, screaming inside. What's the matter with you? Bite his head off, why don't you? What's he going to think now? She kicked aside a clam shell, wishing she could crawl inside and snap it shut.

This was a mistake, Diggon thought as they sped out of the basin. He gripped the handle of the outboard and stared across the glassy surface of the water. There wasn't a ripple.

All the waves were inside the boat. Everyone seemed to be wrestling with something. Everyone but Field. He was the same, perched on the bow as always, singing *Down by the Bay* with verses even more outrageous than the ones last summer. Shouting at the top of his lungs so everyone could hear above the motor, then yelling "Get it? Get it?" until finally Beth turned around and told him to shut up, which of course he ignored.

As for Beth, when she wasn't snapping at Field she was gazing at some point just above Diggon's head. Whenever he caught her eye, she pointedly looked away. Chelsea — "our cousin

from Hawaii," Field had proudly announced —
sat beside Beth and stared blankly at the shoreline,
her hands folded in her lap. She hadn't smiled,
hadn't said a word except to ask about Beth's
knee. No, Diggon remembered, when Field introduced him, her mouth had curved a bit. Maybe
that was her idea of a smile.

Not that *he* was a barrel of laughs. Come to
think of it, he'd barely smiled himself. It was
insane, taking off to the bay as if everything was
normal, as if danger was a game you could play,
with rules you could set, with a beginning and
end you could control.

It had been Field's idea. When Diggon miracu-
lously appeared the day before, Field had practically wet himself with excitement. "Diggon!" he
cried, wading out to meet him, "I don't believe it!
They'll come back for me and I won't be on the
island!" He threw his fishing tackle into the runabout and climbed in. "We thought you weren't
coming. Beth said your place was for sale. We've
rowed over every day to see what was happening, just in case you showed up . . . " Had Field
always talked so much? Diggon wondered. "Let
me off at Billings Spit, OK? Then I can sneak up
on Beth and Chelsea. They're probably on the
beach talking about boys. Or on the verandah
making cranes. They'll think I swam across, but I
won't even be wet! They'll freak!"

When they reached the spit, he hopped out

and said, "See you tomorrow, OK? Right after lunch. We'll row over to your place, then go to the bay for the danger game, just like before. Only now we've got Chelsea, so it'll be even better! She's our cousin from Hawaii and you know what? The other day she swam after the rowboat and — "

"OK, tomorrow," Diggon had said, without thinking it through.

So why are you doing this? The voice hounded him as he guided the boat through the harbour towards Whiffen Spit. *You could have changed your mind. Why the bay?*

Because you see things differently there.

So. You think you'll see yourself differently, like you were before?

Before what?

You know . . .

He bent over suddenly, sick to the pit of his stomach.

"Log!" Field yelled.

"Diggon, watch it!" Beth's voice, loud and frantic.

He gave a sharp turn to the handle but it was too late. The boat swerved abruptly, glanced off the edge of the log, flew above the surface. Everyone clung to the sides to keep from lurching, then braced themselves as the boat hit the water with a heavy smack.

"What are you doing?" Beth shrieked as she

righted herself. "Trying to get us killed? What's the matter with you?"

"Sorry," Diggon said. "I didn't . . . " He shuddered, breathing hard. "Better slow down for a while."

"Whew!" Field used his shirt to wipe the water from his face. "That was a close one. Hey, Diggon. Here's a new verse for the song. Did you ever see a *log?*"

Diggon ignored the barb and concentrated on steering the boat around the spit. There still wasn't a ripple, not even on the strait. He wished he felt as calm.

Beth eased up as they approached the bay. Once, she even looked at him and smiled. And Chelsea, the cousin from Hawaii? Hardly seemed the least bit ruffled when the runabout almost bought it. Just sat there with a solemn look on her face, completely in control. What would it take to shake her up? he wondered. Was she always this calm? Maybe it was just an act. Or maybe — it suddenly struck him — maybe she had what he used to have: the gift of stillness.

Chapter 18

The shoreline along the strait was rugged, marked by bays and coves where the sea had bitten into the land. "Look, Chelsea," Field shouted. "See up ahead?"

She followed his pointing finger and recognized the island Beth had described. But Beth had left out the magic. Mist swirled around the island so it appeared to be floating. Fir trees rose like spires, steep cliffs like the walls of a castle. When Diggon shut off the motor they glided silently through the mist, into the sunlit bay. It even smells like a magical place, Chelsea thought. Sea spray and cedar and sunshine. She breathed deeply. The bay felt good.

"This is it, Chelsea," said Field, leaping off the bow. "Mystic Bay. But I changed it to Watermelon, like in the song." He jumped into the water and pulled the boat ashore, singing, *"Did you ever see a crane with a . . ."*

Beth groaned. "Can't somebody shut him up?"

"Green fingers attack!" he cried suddenly. He picked up a clump of seaweed and squirted Diggon in the face.

"Hey!" Diggon ran over to the rocks and found his own sea sac. He chased Field across the beach, squirting him with jets of water.

"Here, Chelsea! Catch!" A slimy green thing, looking like a hand with puffy fingers, landed at her feet.

"Pick it up and squirt," said Field. "It's only the Sea Sac Monster's hand. He's harmless."

"He only comes out at night," said Beth, chasing after Diggon with her seaweed squirt.

"Then he trades in his hands for new ones, like yours." Diggon spun around, grinned wickedly, and aimed a spray directly at Beth.

"You — " She flew after him and tackled him from behind. Then the two of them were grappling on the ground, trying to squirt each other, trying to roll out of the way, laughing hysterically. "Stop, I can't stand it," Beth pleaded, weak with laughter. "My stomach hurts, stop!"

"Give up?" Diggon kneeled over top of her with the sea sac aimed at her throat.

"Yes, yes!"

He wrenched the seaweed from her fingers and threw it away. Then he reached down to help her up.

"They're in love," Field whispered to Chelsea.

Loudly, he chanted, *"Did you ever see my sister kiss a boy and get a blister?"*

Beth grabbed him in a headlock. "So what danger game should we play? How to torture a brother?"

"No, no! Augghh! You're choking me!" He struggled to loosen her fingers. "Why don't we swim after the boat?"

"What! You didn't — " Beth released her grip and whirled around, expecting to see the runabout drifting away with the tide. But it was securely fastened, right where they'd left it. "Very funny, Slug-brain," she said, shaking a fist.

"I thought so!" He laughed, and jumped out of her range. "I've got another idea. Why don't we play a game with Chelsea?"

"OK, Chelsea?" said Beth. "You want to play the danger game?"

Chelsea looked at their eager faces. An unexpected warmth rushed through her, a delicious feeling of belonging. But somewhere deep inside a voice warned, *Careful, careful, don't get too close . . .*

"Sure," she said, finally. "But why don't we explore first? You can show me all your favourite places. Then we can decide on a danger game."

They showed her the frayed rope swing, the creek with its thin trickle of water, windfalls spanning the gully from last winter's storms, and the hill with the tall grass bleached by the sun.

She followed them into the woods, along a narrow trail leafy with ferns, sprinkled with light and shadow. Bits of sky came through the trees like blue enamel, gleaming through clusters of alder leaves and the lacy branches of cedar. Mossy-grey lichen floated to the ground like witch's hair. A magical place, Chelsea thought. Soft and dark and silent and green. A closed-in, sheltered place, meant for secrets. Not like the lava fields, where everything was open, where spirits could walk and be seen. If there were spirits in these woods, they were well-hidden. "Are there many wild animals here?" she wondered, peering into the grey-green woods.

"Deer, raccoons, mink, take your pick," said Diggon. "We found a cougar track once, by the creek."

"Have you ever seen a cougar?"

"Nope, only the track."

"And there's black bears," said Beth.

"There's lots of no-see-ums," said Field. "You think you see them, but then you don't. Get it?"

"They're actually tiny flies," Beth explained.

Chelsea preferred to think of the no-see-ums as mysterious, phantom-like creatures that lurked in the woods. Behind snags and windfalls, on moss-covered logs, beneath trailing branches, in the still dark pools of the stream. She saw faces in the bark, shapes in the tangled underbrush. But when she blinked, and looked again, they were gone. "Where does this trail go?" she wondered.

"Nowhere," said Field.

"Somewhere," Beth corrected. "All trails go *some*where."

"This one kind of disappears after a while," Diggon said. "But there's a couple of other trails that branch off. One of them goes out to the road."

"Road?" Chelsea was surprised. "This place seems so far from civilization."

"All of East Bracken is far from civilization," Diggon said. "That's what I like about it. But it does have a road."

She pictured the map in her mind. "So we're on the peninsula. Can you get to your place from here?"

"Yeah, but it takes forever. I did it once."

Now Beth was surprised. "I didn't know that. How come you never made that a danger game?"

"It's more fun going back on the water," Diggon said. "And faster."

"And more dangerous," added Field.

Sounds drifted in and out of the woods. Small scatterings, the chatter of a squirrel, quiet rustlings, a splash in the stream. The sudden flap of wings as a bird, startled by their footsteps, flew into the trees. A brushing of needles, the dry snap of twigs. And an odd screaky sound. "What's that?" Chelsea asked.

"Tree trunks leaning together," said Beth.

"You're not scared, are you?"

"Of course not." From somewhere high in the treetops came a deep-throated gurgling, like water bubbling up from a well. "What's that?"

Beth stopped and listened. "Probably a raven. They make all sorts of weird sounds."

"Mostly they sound like crows. *Prrukk, prrukk ...*" Field squawked a raucous imitation. "*Did you ever see a crow ...*"

"Give it a rest!" Beth picked up a fir cone and lobbed it at the back of his head.

"I did a report on ravens once," Chelsea said. "Do you know the stories about Raven the Trickster? He brought light to the world, and fire."

"Cool," said Field.

"Hot, actually," Beth muttered.

Chelsea ignored the interruption. "Once there was a Snowy Owl who lived way up North. He had fire, but he refused to share it. So Raven decided to steal it. He turned himself into a great Deer Chief and told Snowy Owl he would do a special dance for him, but only if he could dance close to the fire, since the owl's lodge was so cold. He spun around closer and closer to the flames until his long tail swirled out and caught fire. He took off from the land of ice and snow with his tail blazing behind him. When he got to the forest his tail torched the trees, one after another. He finally jumped into a stream to put out the fire in his tail."

"Didn't his tail burn off?" Field asked.

"Of course," said Chelsea. "Have you ever seen a deer with a long tail? They have short tails because the fire burnt Raven's tail right to a stump."

"Is that the end of the story?"

"Raven turned back into himself and flew around teaching people how to put out fire with water. Then he showed them how to start it up again by rubbing sticks together."

"I get it!" Field exclaimed. "It's like the fire's still in the wood." He picked up two twigs and rubbed them vigorously. "It's really friction, you know. We've done this before, remember, Diggon?"

"Sort of," he said. "Seems to me it took a long time."

"We could do it again," Chelsea said. "Set the woods ablaze, like Raven. Start a fire and dance around it with branches, as if they were tails. We could act out the whole story, right here in the woods, and see who's the first to start a blaze!"

"Then see who can put it out," said Diggon. "Not likely."

"Oh, come on!" Chelsea urged. "It's not that hard to put out a fire, even — "

"Get real, Chelsea," said Beth. "We're not in Lava Land. We're in a forest, in case you haven't noticed. It's the middle of summer and it's fire season."

"So? All the more reason."

"She's just kidding," said Field. "Aren't you, Chelsea?"

"What do you think?" Chelsea's mouth curved in an odd little smile. Her eyes gleamed with a sense of power.

Is she making fun of us, Beth wondered, or is it a dare? What was behind those eyes? How could she look so — once again, the word *bewitching* came to mind. This time, she didn't laugh it off. She shivered, as if something cold and unpleasant were crawling over her skin.

"Well, Chelsea?" Field persisted. "Are you kidding?"

Chelsea tossed her head so that the heavy mass of hair flowed over her face, hiding her expression. Without answering, she turned and started back towards the bay.

Diggon gave Beth and Field a withering look. "Are you both crazy? Of course she's kidding."

"We knew that," said Field. "We were just testing, right, Beth?"

"Whatever you say." Of course Chelsea was kidding, she told herself. No one in their right mind would play with fire in the woods. But there was something disturbing about her cousin, something . . .

Give it up, Beth. She's still in shock, like Mom said. It's only been a week. We need time to get to know her. To get on like a house on fire. The expression made her shudder. Quickly, she pushed it to the back of her mind. "Hey, Chelsea!" she called, running past Field and Diggon. "Wait up!"

Chelsea turned and smiled, looking about as bewitching as a doorknob.

Right away, Beth felt better. Of course Chelsea was kidding about the fire. They weren't used to her sense of humour, that's all. "Do you know any other Raven stories?"

"Lots," Chelsea said. "My favourite's the one about the fire, but I like the one about the sun and the stars, too. A long time ago . . ."

Beth listened, impressed by the way Chelsea could weave stories together, making one flow into another. The way she could remember stories, period, was amazing. Beth couldn't remember the punch line of a joke, let alone a whole story. "Do you like telling stories?" she asked, when Chelsea finished.

"I like to draw," Chelsea said. "Sometimes I draw stories. It's easier than finding the words, sometimes. When we get back I might draw the story of our trip to the bay."

"I wish I could draw," Beth said. "And tell stories. Or be good at something, period. I'm about as creative as a slug."

Chelsea laughed. "Do you want to hear another one?"

"Sure." Beth listened spellbound, all the way to the end of the trail.

When they returned to the beach, Field wasted no time rummaging through Beth's pack for the cookies and fruit. "I'm starving!" he said, breaking off a handful of grapes.

"What's new?" Beth offered the bag of chocolate chip cookies to the others. "Quick, before he hogs them all."

"Why don't we play the danger game, now?" Field asked between mouthfuls. "You want to, Chelsea? First you have to take the oath and prick your finger like we did."

Once again, Chelsea savoured the feeling of belonging, of being accepted. But again, she heard the voice. Careful . . . Don't get too close. Hard-edged, remember? Soften up, and everything will go wrong.

"It's only a kid's game," said Beth. "No big deal, but it's fun."

Field nodded. "You'll love it."

Not like my kids' games, Chelsea thought. Not like Simon Says. Tear me from the inside out, that's the real danger game. Throw me in icy water, stand me among the wasps, that's nothing.

"Come on," said Beth. "Where's your sense of adventure?"

Careful . . . But what could go wrong? Mystic Bay was a magical place. Like Beth said, you saw things differently there. Maybe it was time to loosen up a little. As long as she could keep things under control. Impulsively, she made a decision. "Sure. Why not?"

They repeated the oath, promising not to tell whatever they saw or heard or did in the bay. "Now we prick fingers," said Field. "Where's your knife, Diggon?"

He took it out and handed it to Chelsea. "Go ahead."

She ran her thumb along the edge of the blade. "It doesn't feel very sharp."

"It's sharp enough," said Field. "Just use the tip. Slice it across your baby finger till the blood gushes out."

"Nice talk," said Beth. "Come on, Chelsea, it's not as bad as it sounds. I'll go first if you like."

Chelsea weighed the knife in her hand. "You know," she said hesitantly, "we could do something different. If you want. To make it special, since there's four of us now."

"Wait a minute — " Beth started to protest, but Diggon cut her off.

"Different, like how?"

Chelsea smiled shyly. "It's just a thought, but . . ." She fished inside her pocket and drew out a box of matches. "We could take the oath of fire."

Chapter 19

Beth stared at Chelsea. Oath of fire? What was she talking about? And where did she get the matches? The box was different from the ones they used at the cabin. So Chelsea must have brought her own. Why? Had she been serious, then, back in the woods? What was she planning now? Beth turned the puzzle around in her head, trying to make sense of it, growing more and more uneasy.

Field had no worries. "An oath of fire!" he exclaimed. "All right! What do we do?"

"You light a match and put your finger in the flame."

"Oh." His face dropped. "Nah, let's do it our usual way."

"Like Beth said, it's not as bad as it sounds," Chelsea continued. "Watch." She struck a match and drew her finger through the flame. "There. You can do it faster if you like. Then you don't feel a thing." She blew out the match. "We could do it with the same flame, one after the other. And if we all do it before the flame goes out, then the oath is fixed. OK?" She looked at them eagerly, her eyes shining with excitement.

"No," Beth said curtly.

The others turned to her, startled by her tone.

"I mean . . ." She tried to sound less forceful, more convincing. "We started the danger game. We should do it our way. Don't you think?" She looked at Field and Diggon for support, but it wasn't forthcoming.

"Where's your sense of adventure?" Diggon asked, repeating her earlier words. "It's different now, with Chelsea. It's equal — two and two. You're not the only girl. We should do something special."

"Yeah, Beth," said Field. "And it won't hurt as much as the knife, probably. Right, Chelsea?"

"I swear you won't feel a thing. As long as you're fast. But your finger does have to go through the flame," she said firmly. "You can't just whizz it across the top."

Field held up his middle finger. "Do we use this one?" he asked with a grin.

Chelsea sighed and shook her head. "Only if you want to be thought of as a Grade Two-er."

He blushed and quickly dropped his hand.

"For a serious oath of fire," Chelsea said, "you have to use your index finger." She held up a match. "Are you ready?"

"Wait a minute!" Beth felt a prickle of panic. "What's going on here? We haven't decided yet! We don't even want to — "

"I do," said Field. "Don't you, Diggon?"

Diggon's eyes flicked from Beth to Chelsea. "Go ahead, light the match. We'll do it."

"Good." She struck the match.

Beth glowered, her thoughts in a turmoil. So Diggon gives the word and right away Chelsea strikes the match. What about me? So I'm not from some fabulous, faraway place and I can't draw or tell stories or swim after boats. Don't I count for anything?

"Move in close," said Chelsea.

Field and Diggon huddled around her. When the flame was burning steadily, she drew her finger through, a slow smile lighting her face. "Diggon?"

With an easy grin, he whisked his finger through the flame. "OK, Field. Your turn."

Field swept his finger through with a bold stroke, like crossing a *t*. "Look!" he said, examining his finger. "It's not even fried. Come on, Beth." He stepped aside to let her in. "The match is almost finished."

She felt their eyes on her, their silent dares more piercing than the prick of a knife. Chelsea was the worst, gazing at her with that maddening smile — why had she ever wanted her to smile? — while the charred matchstick dipped and the flame burned lower and lower. Chelsea didn't care. She seemed completely indifferent to the fact that any second now the flame would burn her fingers.

"Hurry up, Beth," Diggon said. "It's no big deal."

She shot him a look. "Sense of adventure, no big deal . . ." Was he doing it on purpose, deliberately throwing her own words back in her face?

"Yeah, Beth," said Field. "Don't be a chicken."

"No!" Her voice was sharp. "I said it already. No!"

"Are you sure?" Chelsea asked quietly. The flame burned lower.

Field shoved Beth closer. "If you don't do it, Chelsea's going to get burned!"

"So let her! If she's stupid enough to hold onto a burning match without letting go she deserves to get burned."

The expression in Chelsea's eyes hardened slightly. Her lips tightened. Beth lowered her gaze and saw the flame curling around Chelsea's fingers. Quickly, she leaned over and blew out the match. "There. It's finished. I'm not taking your stupid oath of fire."

Field gave her a disgusted look. "You're out, then. I never figured you'd be such a chicken. Did you, Diggon?"

Diggon didn't answer. Maybe she was, maybe

she wasn't. He picked up a small piece of drift-wood, sat on a log, and began to carve. His knife slid easily with the grain. Changing direction, that was the hard part. Going against the grain.

That's what you should have done that night, said the voice. *Just said no, taken a stand, like Beth. When that kid came walking down the side-walk and Blake said "spread out and block him," you should have said no. And when the kid tried to cross the street, you should have stopped Blake from grabbing him and throwing him down and smashing his face against the curb.*

But it happened so fast. I couldn't think, I didn't know . . .

A sudden screech made him look up. A mob of gulls wheeled in frenzied circles above the island, now clear of mist. A bald eagle appeared in their midst, clutching a wriggling fish in its talons. It circled the bay a few times, with the gulls nag-ging in from all sides. Finally it broke free from the mob and soared away. *That's what you should have done,* said the voice. *Broken away and taken the kid with you.*

Beth kicked at a clump of seaweed, her mood fur-ther irritated by the screeching whine of the gulls. Their high-pitched *keer, keer* grated her nerves. Why had they come here? Whose idea was it, anyway? Maybe they should wipe out the day and go home.

She crouched down and rummaged through the beach pebbles, searching for something. A wishing stone or an agate, even a snail shell would do it. Or an arrowhead, though that was unlikely. What she needed now was some sort of good luck charm, even if the significance was all in her head.

It doesn't matter, she told herself. It was stupid, the whole oath thing. Even pricking fingers was stupid. And don't worry, you're not out of anything. Field is all talk. Besides, what does it matter what he says? He's only a stupid brother.

Yeah. So why do I feel so empty, if it doesn't matter?

Get a grip on yourself, Beth. Stop being a wimp. Stick your finger in the flame if you feel that way about it. Chelsea would love to light another match.

It's not the flame, she argued. It's nothing to do with the flame.

She glanced over at Chelsea, sitting beside Diggon with a half-smile on her face, watching as he carved the wood. A tangle of hair tumbled over her shoulders, spilling down her arms, brushing against Diggon's hand . . . Beth felt her muscles clench. Abruptly, she looked away.

Stones, concentrate on the stones. She picked up a black one, smooth as butterscotch, ringed by an unbroken white line. Perfect. She put it in her pocket without showing the others, sadly realizing that any other time she would have shown them her find, exclaiming over it happily, laughing as Diggon teased her about wishing stones and superstitions. A few minutes ago she would have shown Chelsea and helped her find one for herself. Not now.

"I've got an idea for a game," Chelsea said, "if anyone's interested."

"All right!" Field bounded over. "Here? On the beach?"

Chelsea shook her head. "There's a perfect spot at the top of the hill."

"If you're thinking of lighting a fire, forget it," said Beth.

"Don't worry, this has nothing to do with fire." She took the knife from Diggon's hand. "This is the knife game. You don't mind, do you, Diggon?"

"No, but — "

"Good. Come on, then." She ran up the hill with Field close behind.

"Coming, Beth?" Diggon called over his shoulder.

"Yeah, I guess. In a while." She scooped up a handful of stones and sand and watched the grains trickle through her fingers. A knife game? Chelsea hadn't been so keen on knives a few moments ago. Prick our fingers? No, let's burn them instead. Fun and games, Chelsea. What was she up to now? The question nudged Beth up the hill. It was better to know than not to know. At least that way she'd have some small measure of control. Wouldn't she?

At the top of the hill where the trail began, the ground was smooth and level, cushioned by evergreen needles. Chelsea found a stick and drew a circle. "This is what you do. You put your foot inside the circle, while somebody else throws the knife and sees how close they can get it to your foot. See?"

Before anyone could say a word, Chelsea had placed one foot inside the circle and thrown the knife. It landed a hand's width away from her big toe. "Not close enough," she said with a shrug. "Who else wants to try?"

"Is this supposed to be a danger game?" Field asked. "We all have to agree, if it is."

"Sure," said Chelsea. "So do you? Agree, I mean."

"Can't we just do it with our own foot, like you did?"

"Where's the danger in that? You could throw it yards away, so what's the point? This way, you have to trust the other person."

"I'll do it," said Diggon. "If — "

"We haven't all agreed," Field persisted.

"That didn't bother you before," Beth said. "When you took the stupid oath of fire."

"It wasn't stupid. Just because you didn't do it."

"Can't we get on with the game?" Chelsea threw the knife again. This time it came closer to her toe.

"We still have to agree," said Beth. "Just because you brought up the oath of fire doesn't mean we're changing the rules."

Chelsea sighed. "I don't care, all right? You either do it or you don't." She pulled the knife from the ground and aimed at Diggon's foot. "Don't move."

"What? I didn't say — "

The knife spun through the air and landed with a thwunk. "Good one!" Chelsea exclaimed. The blade quivered a finger's width away from Diggon's heel.

"Whoa!" he said. "That was close."

"You can hold it like this with the blade up," Chelsea said, demonstrating. "Then flick your wrist hard so the knife spins over and sticks in the ground. Or you can throw it straight down. Doesn't matter." She grinned. "I was playing this at school once, and the knife went through this guy's running shoe, right between two of his toes."

"Who threw the knife?"

"I did," she said proudly.

"We're not allowed to take knives to school," said Field.

"Neither are we," said Chelsea. "Who wants to go next?"

"Me," said Diggon. "With your foot." He aimed the knife at the foot poised in the centre of the circle. "Ready?"

"Whenever."

Thwunk. "Not bad," Chelsea said. "Could be closer. Come on, Field, you want to try?"

"With your foot?"

"Why not? I trust you. Take a few practice shots, to get the feel of it."

After three practice shots, he threw the knife. It landed on the far side of the circle, nowhere near Chelsea's foot. "Rats! Let me try again."

"I've got an idea," Chelsea said. "Why don't you and Diggon each put one foot in the circle, close together but not touching. I'll throw the knife between them."

"I don't know . . ." Field began.

"You too, Beth. Put your foot in here. The important thing is not to move. You have to stand perfectly still. Frozen, like you were with the wasps, remember?"

"What?" Field scowled at his sister. "You told her about that?" What else had Beth told her? he wondered. About how scared he'd been? It bothered him that Chelsea would know that about him. He might've told her himself, but at least that would've been his choice. "You weren't supposed to tell anything about the bay in the first place," he said angrily. "That's what the oath was all about."

"Things change, don't they?" Beth retorted. "You're not following the rules now, so what difference does it make? You've already ruined the game, all because of Chelsea."

"So." Chelsea fixed her eyes on Beth. "Do you want to throw the knife at me?"

A disturbing silence fell over them.

Chelsea's eyes glittered, but there was no anger there, nothing mean or malicious. It surprised Beth that Chelsea could look so composed. Even her voice was calm, as if she expected Beth to lash out at her in some way, as if the most natural thing in the world would be for Beth to take out her anger by throwing the knife. Worst of all, she acted as if she *wanted* Beth to do it.

Well, she wouldn't. No way would she play into Chelsea's hands. For what? So the others could turn against her even more?

Chelsea's manner confused her. Those eyes, challenging, almost pleading . . . "No," she said, finally. "I don't want — Oh, forget it. Play your knife game; I'm going back to the beach." She walked down the hill through the rustle of grass, feeling a heaviness that had nothing to do with the wishing stone in her pocket.

When she got to the beach, everything had changed.

Chapter 20

Why hadn't she noticed it sooner? "You guys!" she cried. "We've got to get back!"

She put on her life jacket and fastened it with shaking fingers. At the top of the hill, the others were still involved in the knife game. She could hear them laughing and jeering and kidding around, oblivious to the change in the weather. "Hurry up!" she yelled, annoyed by their lack of concern.

Diggon was the first down the hill. "Look at it!" Beth shouted, as if it were all his fault. "It's never been this rough in the bay!"

"How did it get so windy all of a sudden?" he said. "How come we never noticed?"

"I just did! You were too busy with your stupid game. Now what? What if we've left it too late?"

"I love it!" Chelsea slid down the hill and flung her arms out to the waves. "You could almost surf."

"Yahoo!" Field exclaimed. "Let's look for a board."

"Forget it," said Beth. "We're not staying here."

Diggon looked towards the strait. "It's going to be really rough out there. Maybe we should wait it out."

"And get back late?" said Field. "Then we're in trouble."

Beth glared at her brother. "You wanted to stay and surf a minute ago. Anyway, we're in bigger trouble if the boat gets swamped."

"We've got life jackets," Chelsea reminded her.

"Get real, Chelsea. You know how cold this water is?"

"I went swimming in the cove, remember?"

"That's boiling compared to the strait," Beth said. "You can die of hyperthermia if you don't get rescued."

"Hypothermia," said Diggon.

"Whatever."

"Yeah," said Field. "Or you freeze to death."

Diggon took the piece of driftwood from his pocket and started to carve.

"What are you doing?" Beth stared at him, astounded. "This isn't the time to sit back and carve. You're going to *relax* now?"

"Look. We either go and take a chance, right? Or we stay and take a chance. The thing is . . ."

His face was drawn, his mouth set in a hard line. "The thing is, no one knows I'm here. I didn't want to tell you, but — " He shrugged. "If we have to get rescued, that's it."

Beth was shocked. "You mean you didn't come over with your parents? You came by yourself? No one even knows you're at the cove?"

"Cool!" Field gazed at him, his mouth open, his eyes wide with admiration. "Just like *The Fugitive!* Why, Diggon? What did you do, witness a smash and grab or a murder or something? What?"

"I don't want to talk about it."

"Why don't we hike back through the woods?" Field suggested. "That way you can still hide out."

"Oh, brilliant," said Beth. "Do you have any idea how far we are from the cove? Diggon's already said it takes forever to walk there. The trail's probably overgrown. We'd end up lost in the woods."

Field scuffed his toe on the beach, flinging up stones. "You're so smart, let's hear your idea."

Beth looked away. She didn't have an idea, that was the problem.

"Well, Fish-breath?"

"Stop calling me that," she snapped, punching him on the shoulder.

Chelsea stepped between them. "Why don't we try it? In the boat, I mean. Like a danger game."

"You've already had your turn," Beth said. "You can't — "

"Might as well," said Diggon. "It's a good outboard."

"But it's so rough! It's going to be — "

"You've already got your life jacket on," said Field. "See? You're all ready to go."

Beth gripped the edge of the seat. Her white-knuckled hands were cold, her arms stiff with tension. She closed her eyes, trying to think of a prayer, a chant, some words of comfort, but all she could think of was, oh my God, don't let me drown don't let me drown.

Even with the motor going flat out the boat was barely moving. Waves crashed over the bow and against the sides. The boat dropped, plunged, hit the water with a deafening *thwump, thwump* as the sea rose above it. This is insane, Beth thought. They didn't even have a bailing can. Why hadn't anyone checked? She remembered the empty pop cans in her pack and figured they could use those if they had to, if they could pry off the lids somehow, instead of being forced to use the hopeless little holes to bail out water.

She wanted to scream at Diggon to go back, but at the same time didn't want to break down in front of everybody. Especially when no one else looked worried. Field bounced up and down, laughing like a maniac whenever the waves hit the bow. Except for a tightening around his mouth, Diggon actually looked calm.

As for Chelsea, she sat there like some sea goddess, loving the wind and the sea and the danger. Didn't anything bother her? Oh look, there's a drifting boat, I'll just swim after it, doesn't matter how cold the water is. Oh, here's a match, I'll just put my finger in the flame. She's unreal, Beth thought. She's not human.

The whole day was a disaster. Why was everything so out of control? How did it happen? Right from the beginning — no, it was the oath of fire that started it. Before that, everything was fine. Except for Chelsea's idea of setting the woods on fire. But she had been kidding, hadn't she? Beth had overreacted as usual. Same with the knife game. Why hadn't she just gone along with it? The others didn't have a problem. Why had she set herself up for being left out?

And now this. Why was she the only one that was terrified? "Go back!" she screamed. There. The words were out.

Nobody even heard.

Years ago, Dad had taken them on an outing to the far side of the basin. Same thing happened then. Sheltered bay, beautiful beach, happy family picnic . . . and without their noticing, the wind had picked up. Worse, they hadn't come in the cabin cruiser. Dad had insisted on taking the smaller boat with the outboard, to give it one last run before he sold it.

"We can walk back, can't we, Dad? Hike up to the road and walk back to the cabin? Or follow the railway tracks? Can't we?"

"No, no, it'll be fine."

But it hadn't been.

The boat had bobbed in the water like a piece of driftwood, bashed by the waves. "Go back!" she cried.

"It'll be fine."

She had prayed then. She remembered gritting her teeth and repeating over and over *now I lay me down to sleep* . . . ridiculously inappropriate, but the only prayer she knew. When she opened her eyes she saw her father staring grimly across the water, his hands white-knuckled too, trying to steer the boat on a safe course. Then she made the mistake of looking into his eyes and seeing something that scared her more than the wind, more than the whitecaps, more than her fear. *His* fear. She shut her eyes to block out the image. Fathers were not supposed to be afraid.

When they got back, she had flung herself down on the beach, crying, swearing she'd never go out in a boat again, not if there was the slightest hint of a wave, never, never, never . . .

She stared hard at Diggon through the strands of hair whipping her face, willing him to look at her, to smile the smile that would save the day and make her less afraid no matter what happened. The smile that would draw her back in. Her heart leaped as he turned his head.

But he looked right past her and smiled that smile on Chelsea.

Chelsea smiled back. A smile full of daring and excitement. A smile of conspiracy. She wasn't afraid. Neither was Diggon. They were loving it.

It hit Beth then, a feeling more painful than a twinge of jealousy, more powerful than fear. At that moment, she knew what it was to hate.

They were edging through the passage by the island when the motor began to sputter and cough. Suddenly it died.

Beth gripped the seat even harder as the boat rolled in the peaks and troughs of the sea.

Diggon swore, pulled the cord, tinkered with the choke, and pulled the cord again and again. Nothing.

"Maybe we need gas," Field said. "There's a spare can here."

Diggon ignored him and tipped the outboard. "There's the problem. The prop's tangled in kelp." He leaned over to clear it, bracing himself against the wind. "That's got it," he said, once the propeller was cleared. He pulled the cord. The outboard coughed and sputtered again, only this time —

"Smoke!" Field yelled. "It's on fire!"

It can't be, Beth thought, stunned. Oh God, it just can't be. What should they do? Jump out? What?

"Throw water on it," Field cried. "Diggon, do something before it explodes!"

"Relax, would you?" Diggon spoke through clenched teeth. "It's not on fire. It's only steam. The motor's overheated, that's all. Because of the kelp." He pushed his wet hair out of his eyes as another wave splashed over the sides. "We're not going to make it, not now." He looked at Beth and Chelsea. "Trade places with me. I'll row back to the bay."

Still shaking, Beth slid across to the stern, bristling as her cousin squeezed in beside her.

"It was worth a try," said Chelsea.

Diggon pulled hard on the oars and turned the boat around. "Good thing it happened before we got into the strait. At least the wind's blowing us in the right direction."

Beth folded her arms tightly across her chest, wondering what more could possibly go wrong.

The wind pushed them back with astonishing speed. "Now what?" Field asked as they pulled up the boat. "Should we hike back through the woods?"

"And leave the boat here?" said Beth. "Brilliant."

"There's no other way," he persisted, "unless you want to row in the strait."

"It won't be so bad when the wind dies down, will it?"

Beth sneered at her cousin. "What do you know, Chelsea? You can get big swells out there, even when there's no wind."

"Diggon's good at fixing things," said Field. "He can fix the motor. Can't you?"

Diggon was trying, without success. No matter what screws he tightened or how much he fiddled with the choke, the outboard wouldn't start. Finally, after the last futile attempt, he straightened and said, "We'll have to leave it for a while, let it cool down."

"Why don't we build a shelter or something while we wait?" Chelsea said. "Like the windbreak at Tidewater. It's better than sitting around. And the sky's so dark, it looks like it's going to rain any second. That's what happens in Hawaii."

"Tell someone who cares," Beth muttered under her breath.

"I like Chelsea's idea," said Field. "Let's build a windbreak — or a fort! Right by the creek. We'll be out of the wind there. And if the motor still doesn't start, and if we can't find the trail back, we could camp out here like we always wanted to do. That'd be the best danger game, being here after dark. Right, Beth?"

"Shut up." She pushed past him and headed for the creek. Nothing was turning out right. Nothing.

"What've we got left to eat, though?"

"I've got some crackers," said Diggon. "What about you, Chelsea? You got anything?"

She smiled. "I've got matches, remember?"

"You're not going to light a fire!" Beth watched in disbelief as the others gathered small bits of wood. "It's too windy, it'll never go. There isn't any paper. And it's dangerous. It's still fire season, in case you've forgotten."

"That's why we're doing it," said Chelsea. "It's the season of fire."

Beth felt her face reddening with anger. "That's not what — "

"Relax, Beth," said Diggon. "We'll just build a small one, right beside the creek. There's still water, it'll be safe enough."

"Yeah, Beth," said Field. "Stop being such a bummer, OK? Help us get some wood for the fort."

"Forget it." She sat on a log and stared out at the sea. The bay was wild with whitecaps. If anything, the wind was getting worse. The only thing missing was rain. Good, she thought. At least Chelsea was wrong about that.

She watched Field and Diggon drag small logs and planks to the creek bed. "Put a couple on this side, too," she heard Chelsea say. "Lean some wood against the sides so the walls are higher."

Beth shivered inside her windbreaker, wishing she'd brought a sweater like Mom suggested. She swore into the wind, hearing Chelsea give another order. What gave her the right to take charge? This wasn't her territory. She should be the one sitting out in the cold, not Beth. As for Diggon, and her idiot brother, falling all over themselves to please her . . .

"Come inside, Beth," said Diggon. "It's great."

She hauled herself up and moved into the so-called fort. It did keep out the wind, she admitted, although the sound of it wailed through the cracks between the logs.

Chelsea kneeled down and arranged a pile of leaves and lichen. "You don't need paper, not if this stuff's dry enough." She added a few twigs, shredded a clump of witch's hair, then sat back and looked expectantly at the others.

What's she waiting for? Beth wondered. Applause? She was only lighting a stupid fire that the wind would blow out in seconds.

After striking the match, Chelsea held it in front of her face and watched the flame leap and flutter. You'd think she was holding some kind of ceremony, Beth thought. Any minute now, she'll start to chant.

Cupping her hand around the flame, Chelsea leaned forward and lit the tinder. A slow crackle, a blue plume of smoke. She leaned closer, almost touching the flame, then blew on it gently until it flared and took hold.

"All right!" Field exclaimed, adding more wood.

Big deal, thought Beth. She could light fires, too. She'd take all the origami cranes she'd made for Chelsea and burn them right before her eyes. See these? I made them for you. Now they're gone. And she'd laugh at the hurt look on Chelsea's face.

"Have you heard of Pele?" Chelsea asked suddenly. "She's the goddess of fire. She lives in the volcano, on the Big Island of Hawaii. She appears to people sometimes. I've seen her."

"Really?" said Field.

Chelsea smiled at him and nodded. "I found her dog. A puppy, a little white ball of fluff. I was taking him back to the car when I saw a woman walking towards me, across the lava field. First she seemed young, but when she got closer I could tell she was old. Her hair was white and flowed around her face like braided folds of lava. Her eyes burned like fire. She thanked me for finding her dog, then disappeared. Just like that. Then there was a crash. And my dad . . . Well, you know.

"Kawena, my dad's housekeeper, said I was lucky to see Pele. She said it meant something." She made a short sound, not quite a laugh, then bent forward and blew on the flames.

"Get back," said Diggon. "Your hair's going to catch fire."

Chelsea tossed it over her shoulder but did not move back. "I'm not afraid of fire." She held her hands, palms down, above the flames. Taking a deep breath, she lowered them. Slowly, slowly . . . "I don't feel a thing." Her voice sounded hollow and distant.

She stared at the flames trance-like, her face composed and still. Finally she drew back her hands and turned them over. "See? They're not burned."

Field and Diggon shook their heads, not knowing what to say.

Beth looked away, sickened. What would make someone do that? She felt deeply disturbed, not only by what Chelsea had done, but by what she, Beth, had not done. She hadn't pushed Chelsea's hands away. Instead, she had looked on willingly. Horrified, yes, but fascinated, too. Drawn in, like the others, in spite of herself. Bewitched.

A chill passed over her. She uttered a silent prayer that her uncle would get well soon, that he would take Chelsea home and out of her life.

Chelsea got up and casually walked over to the creek. For a long time she held her hands in the cold water, pressing her palms against the coolness of the stones, listening to the water trickling through her fingers, the wind in the trees, the crash of waves on the beach. Listening to the silence of the others, huddled in the fort behind her. So what if they didn't understand? It was all an illusion, really. A trick of the light, the shadow of flames.

Pain was an illusion, too. She could fold it up and tuck it away, inside that secret place deep within her. Anyone watching would think she was brave or crazy or foolish. Never guessing she had simply shifted the pain to another part of herself. The part that was far, far away.

Dad was far away. Was he in pain? Was he awake enough to feel pain, to feel anything? At least he wasn't lost in a coma, helplessly drifting. He was swimming, one powerful stroke after another, struggling to reach the shore. Struggling to reach *her*. She had to believe that. But what about the memory loss, the "post-traumatic amnesia" as the doctor put it? What if he couldn't remember her? What if he didn't know where she was, or worse — what if he didn't care?

If only there was something she could do. Was it enough to make a thousand paper cranes? If she could take on his pain, somehow, would that work?

It was her fault, after all. If she hadn't been in Hawaii, they wouldn't have been going to buy bikes and Dad wouldn't have gotten a flat tire. Not right there. Not then. If she hadn't taken so long getting back to the car, if she hadn't waited out the rain . . . If she could burn away the crash somehow . . .

But there was no way she could undo it. Like everything else, she had to fold that pain and bury it deep inside. She removed her hands from the water and shook them, drying them in the wind before going back to join the others.

Beth watched Chelsea breathe more life into the fire, her breath spinning the flames into images. What was she thinking? Beth wondered. In the nine days she'd been with them she'd never spoken of her home in West Vancouver or her mother. Hadn't even read her mom's postcard. She never mentioned school or friends, unless you could count the report on ravens, and the guy whose toe she almost severed with the knife game. She hardly ever answered questions. Just turned them around somehow so you were the one that ended up answering.

Every morning she was up early, anxiously waiting for news from the hospital. She must worry about her dad, but she never talked about him or the accident. Never talked about what happened before or after. You'd think she'd talk non-stop about Hawaii and how wonderful it was. But no. The Pele story was the most she'd revealed about herself, period. If you could believe it, which was doubtful. What was she hiding?

Suddenly Beth heard herself say, "I've got a new danger game." She looked directly at Chelsea. "We're going to tell secrets."

Chapter 21

Field couldn't hide his eagerness. "Who's going to start? I would, but my secret's probably the most boring. Maybe Chelsea should start, 'cause she's the newest. Agreed?"

Diggon looked up from his carving. "Agreed."

Beth smiled, pleased they were following the original rules of the game. "Well, Chelsea?"

Chelsea held a stick in the flames, waited until the end caught fire, then brandished it like a torch. "It's so easy," she said. "A touch here, a touch there. Then whooosh! Everything up in smoke. Everything burned clean. Everything gone."

"Huh?" Field looked at her and frowned. "That's your secret?"

"No," she said, with a flicker of a smile.

"Well, then?" Beth prodded. "Do you agree? Come on, tell us a secret."

Chelsea blew out the flame and placed the

stick on the fire. "No." Her voice was dangerously quiet. "I don't tell."

"Why not? You must have secrets. Are you afraid of telling? The real danger game is doing what you're most afraid of."

"I said, no."

The edge on her voice surprised Beth. What was the big deal? Why didn't she just make something up, like her Pele fantasy? Why didn't she —

Of course. Suddenly, it became clear. Chelsea was playing a game of her own, a game that she could control. That's what this was all about. Chelsea had no interest in their games unless she set the rules. Well, too bad. "Must be some secret. What did you do? Accidentally kill somebody with your knife game?" Beth smirked, enjoying Chelsea's discomfort. "Did you play your little fire game once too often, is that it? What did you burn down, Chelsea? Is that why your mom took off to Indo — whatever? Did you — "

"Hey Beth, back off!" Field burst out angrily. "Chelsea doesn't have to agree, you know." He turned to Diggon. "How about you? What's your big secret?"

Diggon winced. His face grew taut, his mouth tightened in a thin line. He glanced at Beth, then quickly looked away. "No," he said. "I can't."

"What is this?" Beth shouted. "The danger game's not supposed to be easy, that's the whole point. What's the matter with you? I don't believe you've got such deep dark terrible secrets. What a bunch of wimps."

"You do it then. Tell, tell, tell," Field chanted.

"Stop it," Diggon said sharply.

But there was no stopping him. "Tell, Beth! It was your idea and we all agreed. So tell!"

"Go to hell!" Beth cried. Why were they all turning on her? Why was everything so out of control? She stumbled to her feet, eyes stinging with tears, and rushed outside to the safety of the beach.

"She gets like that," said Field. "You guys are lucky you don't have a sister." There was an awkward silence. "I'll get some more wood."

Diggon handed him his knife. "Cut some cedar branches, too. We can sit on them and use them for blankets later."

Chelsea raised her eyebrows.

"Yeah, blankets," he said. "You've got to keep warm, right? If the wind doesn't die down and if we don't walk back, we might be here all night."

After Field had gone, Diggon pushed the fire together and watched as it flared up again. He listened to the hiss and crackle, a sound that always brought back happy memories. Beachfires in summer, Halloween bonfires, Yule logs at Christmas, made specially by Gran with a magic chemical mix that burned red and green, purple and blue. He'd give anything for a bit of magic right now.

Through the corner of his eye he saw Chelsea lean forward and hold another stick in the flames. At least it was a stick this time. She hadn't really held her hands in the fire, had she? It just looked that way. It had seemed like forever, but it was probably only a second, like when he'd put his finger in the flame.

"Everything up in smoke," she said, interrupting his thoughts.

She turned to him, her immense eyes pulling him in and holding him there. He wavered, then looked away, vaguely disturbed by her intensity. At the same time, he felt drawn to her, strangely comforted by her stillness.

"Everything burned clean."

"Is that what you want?" he asked.

"Is that what *you* want?" she countered.

The question startled him. How could she know? He thought for a moment. "No. Not like that. Not everything gone. Just . . . " He took a deep breath, let it out slowly. "Undone."

"Rewind and erase?"

"Yeah."

"Guess we've got the same problem."

He swallowed hard. "I doubt it."

"Tell me," she said.

To his surprise, he did.

For three days now, every moment of that night had played in his mind, every image, every sound, every feeling, every sour, rotten taste until he thought he'd go mad. Telling it didn't make it go away, but at least it was in the open, not buried inside. And Chelsea listened. Without interrupting, without asking questions, without judging, without looking away. Even her eyes seemed to listen, the gold flecks bright in the firelight, pulling him in, connecting in some inexplicable way.

"No one knew the kid," he said, in a low, choking voice. "There was no reason for it. He was just there, in the wrong place at the wrong time. When it all started I backed away, I stood there frozen, like I couldn't say anything or do anything. It was like it wasn't real, you know? Like something you see on TV only you can't turn it off or switch channels. Next thing I knew there were sirens and people yelling and I took off. And that kid, I wish I'd — " He wiped his eyes. "Beth's right. I'm a wimp on top of everything else."

"No," said Chelsea. "Oh, no." She touched his arm, so lightly she was hardly aware of it happening. But with that one gesture came the urge to touch him again, not with her hands but with her words. "I trust you," she said. "The same way you trust me. And I want — I want to play Beth's game. Now. Just you and me. I want to tell you my secret."

He listened, as she had listened. And when she finished, he yielded to an overwhelming impulse and put his arms around her, not knowing what to say, wanting to stop her trembling, afraid of the secret that weighed down on her, afraid of the hurt. He waited for the wind to blow it away, for the fire to burn it up, for the rain to come and wash it away, all those things that were supposed to happen, and while he waited he held her close.

And that's how Beth found them, moments later, when she returned.

"Here!" she yelled. She hurled the branches she was carrying. Dry tips brushed against the fire and burst into flame.

Chelsea jumped up, pulled the branches out of the way, and stamped out the sparks.

"Sorry," Beth snarled. "Didn't mean to interrupt." She grabbed her pack and stomped out, kicking Diggon as she passed.

"Beth, wait!" Diggon ran after her. "It's not what you think. Beth!"

"You ruined it, you and Chelsea!" she cried. "You ruined everything, you — " Choked by the words, she turned and stumbled up hill, hating him for not following, for not stopping her, hating him for coming back and allowing this to happen, but more than anything, hating Chelsea.

"Beth's gone?" Field dropped his load of branches and handed Diggon his knife. "Where?"

"I don't know. She ran up the hill and took off. She thought me and Chelsea . . ." He shrugged. "I don't know."

"Shouldn't we look for her?" said Chelsea.

"Nah," said Field. "She'll be back." He made himself comfortable on a pile of branches and searched his pack for something to eat. "Chips! I'd forgotten about these." He tore open the bag and stuffed a handful into his mouth. "It must be almost suppertime, you know. You guys want some? They're salt and vinegar."

They waved the chips aside. "Beth might find the trail to the road," said Diggon.

"Yeah, so?"

"So then she could take the road back to Heron Cove."

"That's a long way, she'd never make it."

"And once she got there, she could row home and tell your parents where we are."

"Beth? Row in this wind? No way."

"You're right," said Diggon. "She hates rough water."

"Maybe the motor's cooled off by now," Field said. "Shouldn't we try it?"

"I already did, after Beth took off. It's still the same. I think it's had it." He took the wood from his pocket and carried on with his carving. "If Beth's mad enough . . . If she does row home, then your parents would come in the cruiser and get us, right?"

Field grimaced and drew a finger across his throat. "Game over."

Diggon uttered a dry laugh. "Game's over anyway."

"But you know what?" said Field. "Even if she got back to the cove, by then it'd be dark and no way would she row across the basin in the dark, not by herself." He passed around the near-empty bag of chips. "This is so cool, being here."

Hardly, Diggon thought. Not with those secrets. He'd felt better, telling Chelsea, but now he had her secret, heavier than anything he could have imagined. What do you do with secrets like that?

"Isn't it, Diggon? This is just what we always wanted to do, stay here late."

Not without Beth. What got into her, anyway? Diggon wondered. It wasn't like he was her boyfriend. One kiss on the beach, some letters . . . Still, one of the rules of the danger game was keeping each other safe. He wanted to find Beth, explain what had happened, tell her he was sorry. He didn't want her to be hurt.

He looked up suddenly, feeling Chelsea's eyes on him. "What are you making?" she asked.

"Nothing much." He grinned sheepishly and turned the wood over, looking at it from one angle, then another.

"See how the light's shining on it?" Chelsea

took the wood and held it close to the fire. "It's like a crane. No, one of those long-necked birds I saw by the island."

"Great Blue Heron," said Field. "She's right, Diggon, it looks just like one."

"Could be," he said, taking it back. He hadn't planned on carving a heron, at least not consciously, but now that he knew what to look for he could see it clearly. Maybe some people were like that. They saw in you what they wanted to see, or what they expected to see.

What had Blake seen in him? A loner? A follower? Someone who could be manipulated and forced into situations because he was so desperate to be included? Had he seen Diggon's quietness as a sign of weakness? The awful thing was, he could have been right.

What had Chelsea seen that made her confide in him? Had she caught a glimpse of that other self, the Diggon that could be trusted to do the right thing? Or was it just a matter of "you've told me so I'll tell you"? No. Definitely not with Chelsea. There's no way she would've told him unless she saw something, felt something . . . "Oh, God," he sighed, blinking hard.

"What's the matter?"

He rubbed his eyes. "The smoke. Can't you make a fire without smoke?"

"No," she said. "Can't make one without burning something up, either."

They stared at the flames while Field crunched the remaining chips. "How come you guys are so quiet? This is supposed to be fun." He blew up the empty bag, popped it, and tossed it on the fire. "I'll tell you a secret, something bad I did once. Something Diggon doesn't know."

Diggon laughed. "You, do something bad?"

"I did, I swear it. Even Beth doesn't know. OK, Chelsea? You want to hear it?"

"No. I don't feel like show and tell."

Field kicked at the fire. A frown scrawled across his forehead. Why was she spoiling everything, making him feel like a baby? He'd show her. And Diggon too, the hotshot fugitive. "How about hide and seek?" The instant he said it, he regretted it. What a dumb, baby idea. And guess who would have to hide? They wouldn't even bother looking for him, probably.

"Good idea," said Chelsea.

He knew it. Now she'd tell him to get lost.

"And Diggon has to hide," she continued. "We cousins have to stick together, right?"

"Huh? What?" He couldn't believe his ears.

She smiled at him and he grinned back, ridiculously happy. "OK, Diggon? You're going to hide?"

Diggon concentrated on his carving, cutting flecks in the wood to texture the heron's feathers. His brow creased with thought.

"Diggon? Are you listening?"

"Yeah . . . OK, sure. I'll give the outboard

another try, then I'll go look for Beth. You guys can find both of us. Give me a five-, ten-minute start."

"We don't have a watch."

"Then wait till the fire dies down."

"What if you can't find Beth? What if she's walked back?"

"Relax, Field. I think I know where she is."

Chapter 22

Beth stormed along the trail, furious with Chelsea, with Diggon, with herself, with her whole life. She brushed away the tears, cursing the kelp and the motor and the wind that totally destroyed the day. And wonderful Chelsea's oh-so-wonderful fire. It would've been fine if it hadn't been for Chelsea, if they hadn't got stuck here, if they could've gone back in the boat like normal. If the others hadn't broken all the rules and shut her out.

Why had she told Chelsea about the danger game? After swearing she'd never tell, she'd told her everything, the oath, the games, worst of all, how she felt about it. It was her own fault things had gone so badly. Chelsea wouldn't have started those games if Beth hadn't led her into it. She could tell Diggon wasn't that interested, and Field, well, they could have laughed him off as a ten-year-old joke. But no, she had to draw

Chelsea in. Wanted to! That was the amazing part, she *wanted* to bring her inside their circle. She wanted Chelsea to share their secret and the forbidden territory of the bay. She had enjoyed showing her the island and the cove, even though she'd been uncertain at first. She had actually liked Chelsea! And she wanted Chelsea to like her.

There. She admitted it. She had wanted Chelsea to like her, to like Tidewater and Mystic Bay, to feel as if she belonged.

Chelsea belonged, all right. Beth was the one driven out.

She followed the trail deeper into the woods, lowering her head against the shower of evergreen needles and hemlock cones blown down by the wind. Why did she care? Chelsea would only be staying a short time, then she'd be gone. She'd probably go back to being the unknown cousin she'd always been. So why did it matter?

Because Chelsea was different. Because she was clever and creative and had shown glimmers of being a fun person. Because she was adventurous in ways Beth had never dared to be.

It mattered because she was her cousin. There was a link, no matter how — what was that word? — tenuous. And because there was something about her Beth wanted to know and understand.

It mattered because of that moment on the beach when Beth had given her the rumpled crane and Chelsea had held it as if it were the most precious thing in the world.

But she was crazy! Sticking her hands in the fire — how could a normal person do something like that? And throwing her arms around Diggon, how could she?

That image unleashed a new torrent of anger. "I'll show you, Diggon. And you, Chelsea. Just wait. Who cares about your stupid secrets anyway? You're just weird. And sick." She spat out the words. "Sick, sick, sick."

She passed the spot where they'd turned back earlier and the trail that led to last summer's wasp nest. How far was it to — She stopped suddenly, her heart pounding. Where was she going?

Great, Beth. Typical. Blundering off without a clue. She peered into the darkening forest. A little ways ahead and to the right she spotted a familiar shape, a giant fir once hit by lightning, now a snag, rising like a steeple. She struggled through the leafy salal and shoulder-high ferns until she reached the dead tree.

The trunk was hollow, burnt out by fire. A crack on one side was barely large enough to squeeze through, but once inside there was room for three to sit comfortably. Although now, as she looked around, the space seemed smaller. Cracks let in splinters of light. Black peaks, like shards of glass, pointed to the jagged opening. She could look up and see the sky, streaked with scudding clouds.

She and Diggon had discovered the snag last summer, the one time they had come to the bay without Field. The cavern, they called it. Who had crawled through the sword ferns and found it first? It didn't matter.

The cavern marked a first, though. First time without Field. And more importantly, the first time she and Diggon held hands. Here, right in the hollow tree. "Your hands are sure small," Diggon had said.

She had held them up, studying them, turning them this way and that. "Look about right to me," she said. "Why? How big are yours?"

"Huge!" He held up one hand, pressed it against hers, palm to palm. "See what I mean?" The tips of her fingers barely reached his first knuckle.

"Well yeah . . ." she stammered, feeling her face grow hot.

"Really small." He gave her a slow smile and clasped her hand. Held it for a long time, in the cavern and all the way back to the beach.

She remembered how warm and strong his hand felt. How her feet hadn't touched the ground for days afterwards.

So much for flying, she thought, as a new stream of tears poured down her cheeks. She fished in her pocket, took out the damp remains of a Kleenex, wiped her eyes, and blew her nose. Come on, Beth. Think of something else.

Leaning against the charred trunk, she pulled her knees up to her chest and contemplated her hands, the webbing of creases, folds, and lines on her palms. Life line, head line, heart line. And that line crossing the heart line, the destiny line, what did that mean? The arrival of Chelsea probably, coming to screw up her life.

She sighed and dropped her hands in her lap. Why had Diggon come back? She'd wished for it so hard, so often, but not like this. He was supposed to come back and make everything the same as it used to be, only better. And there wasn't supposed to be Chelsea.

She tried to decide her next move. Go back to the beach and join the others? Find the trail to the road and go home on her own? Stay put until something happened to make up her mind? It was so hard to think with the wind whining through the trees and whistling through the cracks in the cavern. The sound was eerie and unsettling, and did nothing to calm the miserable tangle of feelings twisting inside.

Chapter 23

"Was that true, that story you told about Pelly?"

"*Pay lay*," Chelsea corrected. "Of course it was true. And here's the proof." She opened the zippered pocket of her pack and took out a book.

"Is that a diary?"

"Sort of. I call it a journal." She flipped through pages of sketches, maps, and words until she came to the one marked July 14. "See this?" Words were scrawled across the page, written heavily in black ink.

Field leaned forward. "Your writing's hard to read."

"Not the words, this!" She pointed to something tucked along the edge, almost lost inside the binding.

"It looks like hair."

"Exactly." She removed it so he could see the small cluster of white hairs, carefully tied together with thin black thread.

"I don't get it."

"Oh, Field." Chelsea gave him a disappointed look. "I thought we were kindred spirits."

"Well, yeah, we are." He frowned, wondering what she meant. "But they're just hairs, like — Ah!" His face cracked in a grin. "Now I get it! They're from Pele's hair, when she turned into an old lady, right?"

"Close," Chelsea said, "but not exactly. They're hairs from the puppy. Remember I told you I found him? And was carrying him back to the car? Well, when I got home after the accident I noticed the white hairs on my T-shirt. And I thought, there's the proof! So I brushed them off and managed to find some longer ones to tie together. Then I put them inside my journal so I could show Dad."

"You're so lucky," Field said wistfully. "I wish I could see something like that. I thought I saw a ghost once, down by the boathouse, you know? But it was only fog. Do you believe in ghosts?"

"I believe in spirits outside myself and inside myself. Sometimes I feel as if part of me is in a different place, watching the part of me that's left behind."

"Wow," Field said. "I wish I could do that."

"You can. All it takes is concentration. You know when you took the oath of fire and put your finger through the flame?"

"Yeah . . ."

"It didn't hurt, did it?"

"No . . ."

"You see? When I held my hands in the fire I didn't feel anything 'cause I put the feeling part of me in a different place."

"Cool! Know what? I saw this show once — "

"Sometimes," Chelsea continued, "my mind goes far away." She took a pencil and began drawing flames in her journal, transforming them into the flickery images of mythical beasts. Some were hideous and demon-like, with bulging eyes and pointed fangs, while others appeared gentle, their flame-shaped wings flowing across the page like streams of water. "Sometimes I look back and see my body and it's as if it doesn't even belong to me. And if it doesn't belong to me, then I can't feel anything that happens."

"But I don't — "

"Nothing can hurt me. Sometimes I don't even look back. And later, I burn it all up. Whoosh!" Before Field could stop her, she ripped out the page and tossed it into the flames. "All gone. All up in smoke."

"That was a good picture, Chelsea! You should've — "

"Why don't you try it? You'll see what I mean. Try one hand, for a second. And you don't have to hold it that close to the fire. Just as close as you like." She smiled. "Oh, one thing . . ." She leaned closer and bent her head so her hair brushed against his face. Lowering her voice, even though there was no one else to hear, she whispered,

"Please don't say anything about my journal. Or the dog hairs. It'll be our secret, OK?"

"Sure, Chelsea. I swear." He breathed in the scent of her hair, the scent of cedar and sea-salt and something else, a sweet fragrance he thought must be tropical. He felt his cheeks grow hot. Abruptly he straightened, disturbed by her closeness for reasons he did not understand. "I swear," he repeated. "I'll do anything."

Her eyes glittered. "Let's start with the fire."

He nodded and held out his hand.

Not too close to the flames, not to start with. The flames were dying down anyway, not leaping and dancing like they'd been a while ago. But the wind could whip them up at any moment, whip them into a frenzy, especially with a hand held out, palm side down.

He held his hand high above the fire. Willed his mind to go somewhere else so he wouldn't feel a thing. But where? What was Chelsea talking about? If you put your hand in the fire it would burn. It would hurt, no matter what you were thinking. He'd accidentally touched enough red-hot roasting sticks to know that. And had mistakenly stepped on a burning ember in his bare feet. That hurt!

He didn't understand what Chelsea meant. Looking back at your body as if it wasn't yours? But it *was* yours. It *would* hurt.

"Do you want some help?" she asked. "I could

hold your hand and we could do it together, if you don't think you can do it by yourself."

"No, no. I can do it. I'm putting my mind somewhere else, first." Of course he could do it. It wasn't as if he was going to stick his hand in the fire and keep it there. No way would she have to hold his hand like a baby. And maybe this was a way to get back at Beth. He'd seen how upset she was when Chelsea put her hands in the fire. If he could do it too, he'd show her. He'd have some power over her then, doing something that she couldn't.

He felt Chelsea's eyes on him. Glancing over, he noticed how bright they were, how dark and bright at the same time. He remembered how Beth had described those eyes, how they looked as though they could leap out and pull you in. But pull you in where?

Somewhere mysterious. Somewhere wonderful. After all, Chelsea had talked to a spirit. A fire goddess! And she'd told him her secret about the journal and the dog hairs. Not Beth, not Diggon, but *him*, even though he was the youngest. She trusted him to keep that secret. One hand in the fire was a small price to pay for that trust. Of course he'd do it. Chelsea knew what she was talking about, even if he didn't understand. He'd show her he wasn't a baby.

Swiftly, he plunged his hand into the flame. In and out, as quick as a breath. "I did it!" he exclaimed. "It worked! I kept thinking, this fire is ice and I didn't feel a thing!"

"What did I tell you?"

"I'll do it again!" And he did. Quick plunge in and out. "See? I bet I can hold it in longer, this time. Watch."

"Wait," she said, putting a hand on his arm. "Do you want to play a *real* danger game?"

"All right!" He beamed.

"Come on, then."

He followed her away from the fire and onto the beach. "Shouldn't we look for the others first? It's been more than ten minutes."

"I don't think so. The fire hasn't burned down that much. Anyway, do we really want to find them?"

"No way," he laughed.

"First we need some driftwood, about this size." She picked up a piece the length of her arm. "Nothing bigger, OK? And about this wide." She held her hands a ruler's length apart. "Try to get thick pieces, 'cause we want them high off the ground."

"What are we going to do?"

"You'll see," she said. "Get about six pieces and bring them here."

Field set off along the beach gathering driftwood and humming to himself. Chelsea checked each piece carefully, then arranged them to form a circle.

"Is this like the knife game?" he asked.

"Much, much better."

When the circle was complete she stepped back to admire her work. "Perfect. Just the right size. It's important, you know, to get things right."

"Now what?"

"Now you stand inside the circle." Her eyes gleamed.

He raised his eyebrows in a question, then shrugged and jumped inside. "If you say so. Now what? I jump back out? That's easy. In and out and in and out. This is some game, Chelsea." He laughed.

"It gets better." She walked over to the boat —

"I can even do it on one foot. See?"

— and came back with the spare can of gasoline. "No matter what happens, stay inside." She unscrewed the cap and began pouring gasoline over the driftwood. "Don't leave the circle."

He grimaced at the stink of fumes. "What's Diggon — "

"Hey, Cousin," she said with her slow smile, "we've got one secret, remember? This can be another one."

"All right!" He was pleased she would trust him with another secret. Now he could really show Beth. And Diggon. At the same time, he felt uneasy. What was she doing? Gasoline? She wasn't really thinking of —

"Now. How adventurous are you?"

"I'm *really* adventurous. Remember when I

said I had a secret to tell? That even Beth didn't know? Well, there was this — "

"I believe you." Her eyes bored into his as if she were skewering him like a marshmallow on a stick. He blinked and looked away. For one wild moment, he wished the others would return.

"Don't look so worried." Chelsea gave him a warm smile. "I thought you were an adventurous spirit, like me."

"I am! But — "

"Don't you trust me? I mean, *really* trust me? You know I'd never do anything to hurt you. 'Cause that's part of the oath, isn't it?"

"Sure, Chelsea. I trust you."

"And you'll do anything? For the danger game? For me?"

He nodded. Of course he would. What else? There was no question of stepping outside the circle, of not seeing it through, whatever *it* was. After all, she —

It happened so fast. The match in her hand, the quick rasp as it struck the side of the box. The sudden realization. The sound of his voice, dazed, incredulous, barely recognizable. "You're not going to —"

WHOOOMP

The gas exploded, circling him with flames.

Chapter 24

"Beth! Where are you?"

The sound jolted her awake. For a moment she struggled to remember where she was. Then it all came back, the hurt, the anger, running off into the woods, falling asleep in the cavern.

"Beth!"

It was Diggon's voice. She could hear him crashing through the underbrush, heading towards the snag. She rubbed her eyes and crawled outside. "I'm in here," she said, stretching her cramped muscles. "I mean, I was in there, but now I'm out here and — Oh, forget it." Why couldn't she keep quiet? Or say the right thing?

"It's OK," he said, smiling. "I figured you'd be here."

"You did? Really?" Beth, shut up. Don't sound so pathetically eager. You're furious with him, remember?

He brushed his hand against the back of her

windbreaker. "There's black stuff all over it."

"From leaning against the burnt wood, I guess." She didn't care. It was enough to have him touching her, feeling his hand on her back and shoulders even if it was just a brisk, unromantic brushing away of charcoal.

"That's the worst of it," he said, lowering his hand.

Now's the time to talk to him, Beth decided. If she made the first move, then he would explain and apologize, too. "Look, Diggon. I — "

"Come on, the others are waiting." He pushed ahead through the ferns.

"Yeah, right." So much for apologies, she thought bitterly. "We wouldn't want to keep Chelsea waiting."

He ignored her remark. "Either that or they're out looking for us. Field's hide and seek danger game." He held back the branches of salal so she could pass through more easily. "They're probably farther down the trail, coming to find us."

"Maybe they've taken off in the boat," Beth said. "Chelsea's crazy enough to do anything."

"It's not what you think, you know. She's got — "

"Problems? Who hasn't?"

"No, seriously. The thing is . . ." He paused, searching for the right words. "When you were gone, Chelsea and I — "

"I know what you and Chelsea were doing. Spare me the details, OK?"

"It's not what you think," he repeated. "When you were gone she told me something. She was really upset. I can't tell you — "

"She told you her big secret, is that it?" Beth said angrily. "You and Chelsea played the game you wouldn't play with me. I suppose you told her your big secret, too. Right?" Her voice sounded too loud, too frantic, but she couldn't bring it down. "Why did you come over here on your own? Are you running away from something or what? Why won't you tell me? What's — "

"Hold it!"

"I suppose Field knows everything!"

"No, he doesn't. Look, sometimes it's better not to know, all right?"

"Not when everybody else knows," she shot back. "It's not better when you're the only one left out." It was all wrong, the way it was going. She had wanted to explain, say she was sorry, and have Diggon do the same. Instead they were locked in a shouting match, something they'd never done before, with her coming on like a raving idiot. "I suppose Chelsea — "

"Just try to — "

"Yeah, right. Try to understand. Poor Chelsea's got problems. That's brilliant, Diggon. It doesn't take a genius to figure that out."

"She's not what — "

"Shut up about Chelsea!" Beth hurled the words in his face. "OK? Shut up!" She spun around and hurried along the trail, trying to hold back the new rush of tears that threatened to spill down her cheeks.

There was no sign of Field or Chelsea. Not on the trail, not behind trees or hidden in the underbrush. Probably still in the fort, Beth thought. Hopefully still in the fort. Hopefully not rowing in the strait. That would be typical of Chelsea. Oh sure, I can row back, no problem. And Field — sure, Chelsea, let's row back without the others, anything you say. What wonderful little secrets had she told him after Diggon had gone? And what had Field told her? Stuff about Beth, probably. All that stuff about her and Diggon. And what he didn't know, he'd have great fun making up.

When did this trail get so long? she wondered. She was half-running, anxious to get back, when Diggon suddenly cried, "Beth, look!"

She stopped, frightened by the alarm in his voice.

"Where's that smoke coming from?"

She hadn't noticed it before, the cloud of smoke rising from the direction of the bay. It wasn't coming from the creek where Chelsea had lit the fire — no, this smoke seemed to be coming from the beach, right beneath the hill. She broke into a run, telling herself it was only a small fire, there were no trees on the beach, it was safe enough, but she could feel the panic building up and rising, black and terrible as that smoke.

She reached the top of the hill and looked down.

And saw her brother, standing in a circle of flame.

He hadn't meant to scream. He'd meant to be brave, worthy of the ultimate danger game, worthy of Chelsea's trust. He'd felt he could be brave, could do anything with Chelsea there, watching. He wanted to impress her, to brag about it, to tell Beth and Diggon that he and Chelsea had done something *really* dangerous, and they hadn't.

But this!

He stared at her, speechless with shock. And she stared back, her lips curled in a smile, repeating the words, "Trust me. It's all right."

How could she do this? How could she do this and *smile?*

The wind swept the flames closer. Whipped them into a whooshing rush, fuelled by the gasoline, circling, circling . . .

There was no way out, except to run through the ring of fire. But what if he tripped and fell? What if some gas had accidentally splashed on his running shoes or his socks, and a spark touched it off? What if his clothes caught on fire, or his hair? Was that singed hair he smelled?

No matter what happens, don't leave the circle. That's what Chelsea said. That's what he agreed to. Whatever you do, don't move. But could he move, even if he wanted to? It was the wasp day all over again. He felt them crawling over his skin and under his skin, only this time there wasn't a wasp in sight.

Blood thudded in his ears. Don't panic, he told himself. The gas will burn off, the flames will die down. But when? How long will it take? And if the wind keeps blowing them closer . . .

He stood frozen, feeling the heat, too terrified to move. While Chelsea stood entranced, a half-smile on her lips, her eyes wild and bright as they followed the frenzied leap and quiver of flames.

A horrifying sound, something between a strangled shriek and a roar, erupted from the top of the hill. He turned his head and saw Beth tearing down the hill, her face contorted with rage.

She threw herself at Chelsea and knocked her to the ground. Then, in one quick, violent movement, she reached across the fire, grabbed Field's arm, and pulled him through the flames. "How could you?" she yelled. "How could you be so stupid? Don't you know she's crazy?" She shook him by the shoulders. "How could you let her do this? You were nearly burned! You — "

"Ow, Beth, you're hurting . . ." He broke loose from her grip, unsettled by her anger. Turning away, he saw Chelsea stumble to her feet. She stood with her head bowed, raking her fingers through her hair so it lifted and fell, lifted and fell, flowing like curtains over her face. The sight of her, like that, unsettled him even more.

"It wasn't as bad as you thought, Beth. Honest." He tried to hide his confusion. "It was scary at first, but I knew it was OK as long as I stayed inside the circle. See? The flames are dying down already. And I concentrated on something else, like Chelsea told me." Why was he sticking up for her? It was terrible what she had done. But at the same time, he'd got Beth a good one. Now she knew how mad and scared and frantic he'd felt when she rowed away and left him alone on the island. And it wasn't all Chelsea's fault, was it? He'd had a choice. "She didn't force me you know, it was a danger — "

"That's enough!" Beth snapped. She scraped together a handful of wet sand and pebbles and threw it on the wood, helping Diggon smother the flames. "Do you know what this looked like from the top of the hill? It looked like *you* were on fire. How do you think I felt? What's Dad going to say?"

"We can't tell," said Field. "Those are the rules."

"What rules? You stopped following the rules with that oath of fire, remember? The danger game is *over*. Understand?" She whirled around to Chelsea. "Understand, Chelsea? Concentrate on that!"

She paused, breathing hard. "We're going to

walk back to Diggon's and go home in our boat. The runabout will be safe here. Dad can come and get it tomorrow."

"Diggon could try the motor again," Field said.

"No," she said decisively. "Even if the motor starts, it's still too rough in the strait. You guys make sure the fire by the creek is out. And this one." She kicked a piece of smouldering wood into the water. "And don't forget the life jackets. We'll need them crossing the basin."

"Beth?" Chelsea said hesitantly. "There wasn't any danger. I've done it before. And Field — "

"Stop it!" Beth's voice cut her like a knife. "You can play whatever games you like, but you leave my brother out of it. Leave us all out of it. We never wanted you here. We never wanted you, period."

So what's new? Chelsea thought as she stamped out the last few sparks. Flare up, die down. Flames and ashes. It's always the same.

But what's their problem? she wondered, keeping her distance as she followed them along the trail. Diggon had raced down the hill after Beth and immediately started putting out the fire. Not a word to her, not then, not since. Not even a glance in her direction. As if she were suddenly invisible.

And Field? One minute he was trying to defend her, the next minute he was treating her like a three-eyed monster.

As for Beth, she'd started the danger game in the first place. She'd told Chelsea how much she loved it. If Diggon had come up with the ring of fire she would've been all for it. That was her problem though, wasn't it? It had nothing to do with Chelsea. It had everything to do with Diggon.

So. Take it out on me, Beth. I'm used to it.

She took out a match, struck it, and blew out the flame. Sucking in a breath, she pushed up her sleeve and held the glowing matchstick to the inside of her arm.

"There," she said, looking at the tiny red circle. "That's for being Chelsea." The other marks were so faded, she could barely make them out. For a while, she had actually thought the fires had stopped burning.

Chapter 25

It was dark by the time they stumbled onto the road. Beth sighed with relief, thankful to be out in the open, away from the claustrophobic darkness of the woods.

Moonlight spilled through the trees, making shadows on the road. The wind rustled the branches, soft whisperings stirred up now and then by sudden gusts. She wished it would die down completely. She wished she could put it out, like a fire. It made her head feel crazy the way it whirled up her thoughts, as if it were blowing inside her mind. She wished she could shut it out.

She concentrated on the footsteps around her. Diggon, Field, Chelsea. All of them keeping the same rhythm, the same pace. What was going on in their minds? Better not to know.

Their silence hurt. She wanted voices, laughter, the way it was before, when they first arrived at the bay. Now even Field was silent.

He hadn't been earlier when they were still on the trail. He had picked up a stick and hit bushes and trees as he passed, a heavy thwack, thwack, in rhythm with his footsteps, in rhythm with the tune he started singing under his breath.

Beth had kept her eyes on his slight figure, trying not to watch Diggon, way up ahead, trying not to think about Chelsea, far behind.

> *Down by the Bay* . . . Thwack thwack
> *Where the watermelons grow* . . . Thwack thwack
> *Back to my home* . . . Thwack

She wanted desperately to get home, to get away from Mystic Bay. Where you see things differently.

Had she really said that?

Yes, but she'd meant it as a joke. *Did you ever see a bear with purple underwear?* Silly rhymes, kid stuff. Fun stuff, like the danger game was supposed to be. *Exciting* dangerous, without going over the edge. Look what it had turned into. This monster, Chelsea. How could she fold paper cranes and talk like a normal person one minute, and the next minute practically set a kid on fire?

You see things differently all right. But she'd never thought it would mean seeing herself differently. She couldn't believe how she'd suddenly made a decision and taken charge. For the first time she saw herself as someone who could be strong. A lonely outcast, she added melodramatically, but strong.

How did Chelsea see things? she wondered. She shuddered at the thought. At the same time, she realized that in spite of everything she really did want to know. It astonished her, that she could still care. But she'd never let Chelsea know it.

Although the wind had died down, it was by no means still. Treetops swayed overhead. A branch cracked, then hit the ground with a heavy thud. Sudden gusts rained down hemlock cones and sprays of cedar. Fir tree needles blew everywhere. She shuddered again, realizing it wouldn't be calm on the basin. There was more rough water ahead. But then she'd be home, and this hideous day would —

"Beth? Are you OK? I'm sorry if . . . "

She refused to turn around. She shut out the sound of Chelsea's voice and that of her brother muttering *Did you ever see a trail* . . . or whatever. She concentrated on pushing her way through the tunnel of salal.

It wasn't easy. The trail was so overgrown she could barely make it out. Branches scratched her hands and bare legs. Leaves sawed across her face. She had lost all sense of direction. They could be circling back to the bay for all she knew. "Diggon, wait!" she called. "Are you sure we're on the right trail? Diggon!"

Ahead, Diggon had stopped.

"What happened to the trail?" Beth said. "Did we miss something or what?"

"I tried to tell you," said Field. "Didn't you hear me? I kept saying, *did you see that trail?* There was another one back there that went off to the left. You guys should've stopped. Now we're probably lost." He faced Beth with an accusing look. "We should have stayed at the bay. We built a great fort there. We should — "

"We're not lost," Diggon said sharply. "I've come this way before, OK? The trail's overgrown, that's all."

They struggled through the dense growth of bushes, through dark green ferns, through a patch of mucky black soil ripe with the unmistakeable odour of skunk cabbage. They stumbled over fallen logs, through prickly stands of Oregon grape. Finally, after fighting their way through a tall thicket of salmonberry, they had reached the road, exhausted.

Field looked up at the moon and yawned noisily. "How much farther?" he asked, breaking the silence.

"Not far," Diggon said.

"Can't we phone Dad to pick us up?"

"Get real," said Beth. "Do you see any houses? Any phone booths?"

"No," he sighed.

"Only one way back now."

Field took a swipe at the bushes alongside the road. "Yeah. Walk, walk, walk. Then row, row, row."

And maybe, Beth thought hopefully, maybe by then the basin will be calm.

"There's no one here." Diggon shone his flashlight down the empty driveway. "No tire tracks, nothing."

"You sound disappointed," said Chelsea.

He wondered about that, as they staggered down the steps to the beach and collapsed on the dock. Was he disappointed? Had he been half-hoping his parents would be here, waiting to take him home?

Yes, he admitted. That's probably why I came to the cove in the first place. But it didn't work, did it? They probably haven't even missed me.

After three days? Of course they've missed you. What day was it, Monday? No, Tuesday. They would've expected you home from CJ's last night. Probably phoned the cops when you didn't show up. And don't forget, all those new buddies of yours will be phoning, asking where you are. And that kid, remember —

Shut up!

Remember that kid? Cops will be asking a lot of questions. Maybe those new buddies of yours —

Shut up! They're not my buddies. I hardly even know them.

— maybe they've already ratted on you. Said they saw you, given your name. And there were other kids at that party who saw you leave, maybe even saw —

Shut up!

Diggon clenched his fists and pressed them against the sides of his head, trying to stop the shaking, hoping the others wouldn't notice. Would it always be like this? Would he ever be free of it?

"Hey, Diggon," Field said. "You don't have to come with us. You could hide here all summer and we could bring you food. We wouldn't tell anybody. Are you sure you want to come to our place?"

"Yes. Yes!" he repeated emphatically. Beth was right. The real danger game is doing what you're most afraid of. Facing up to the terrors in your head.

But then —

Shut up!

— then you have to face the consequences.

Yes. Maybe then, the voice would leave him alone.

Beth listened to the waves slapping against the dock and the rowboat. As long as she didn't look at the water, as long as she didn't see the white-caps, she'd be OK. But there was no sense putting it off any longer. It could get worse before it got better, as Dad always said. Great time to think of him, she thought grimly. He'll be in some sweat by now. "We've got to go," she said. "And I'm going to row. It's better if I do something."

"I'll help," Chelsea said. "If you like. It might be easier with two of us, unless . . ."

Her words hung in the air.

Beth felt her body grow tense. The last thing she wanted was Chelsea's help. To sit beside her on that seat, arms and legs touching . . . On the other hand, with two of them rowing they would get back faster. Diggon looked so totally out of it there was no point even asking him. And he hadn't offered. "OK," she said. "As long as you keep time with me. Otherwise we end up — "

" — in circles. I know." Chelsea squeezed beside her on the middle seat.

They set the oars in the oarlocks while Field untied the boat and pushed it away from the dock. The boat lurched and rocked, battered by the waves, until Chelsea and Beth each gripped an oar with both hands and began to pull. "Keep together," Beth said impatiently. "Harder, Chelsea. We're not going anywhere. You've got to be as strong as me. Otherwise, don't bother."

"I'll get it, don't worry." Chelsea tightened her grip and pulled. The boat surged ahead. They bent forward in unison, pulled back together. "I'm getting it," Chelsea cried as the bow broke through the waves. "I've got it. We've got it!"

Beth concentrated on rowing. Her hands and

face were wet and cold, her lips tasted salty. The sting of salt bit into the scratches on her legs. The muscles in her arms and legs ached, but she didn't let up. The more they ached, the faster they'd go, the sooner they'd get out of this mess. They were well past the island, out of the cove, heading into the worst part, into the basin where the wind would be the strongest.

A powerful gust whirled the boat around and sent a wave smashing over the bow. Beth screamed, "Hang on, Chelsea! Don't lighten up now! Pull!" Harder, harder . . . She felt a dull ache in her lower back, a sharp pain in her stomach. Oh God no, not cramps, not now. "Chelsea, hang on!"

The boat spun wildly, one minute high on the crest of a wave, the next minute plowing into a trough. The sea spilled over the sides. Her feet were soaked, almost completely covered by water. Much more of this and the boat would be swamped. They'd all be thrown out. It was insane, the rowboat was too small, they never should have tried it. Three of them maybe, not four. But it was too late to think of that now. "Diggon!" she yelled.

He sat in the stern like a block of wood, his eyes fixed blankly on some point in the distance. What was the matter with him? "Diggon!" There was a desperate edge to her voice. "Start bailing!"

He gave her a startled look.

"There's a bailing can under the seat. Don't

just sit there! Do something!"

Her words jolted him. He reached for the can and frantically started bailing as the water continued to pour over the sides.

How long could they keep this up? Surely they were almost there. How much farther was it, anyway?

She made herself look up and instantly regretted it. Moonlight caught the whitecaps frothing against the blackness. A terrible blackness that went on and on. When did the basin get so huge? She looked over her shoulder and saw lights in the distance, flickering at irregular intervals along the shoreline. They must be cabin lights, and one of them must be theirs, but which one? And why were they so hazy?

She strained her eyes, trying to recognize landmarks. Those dark shapes looming above the water must be pilings, so that would be the wharf, in which case their beach would be farther to the left . . . A low sound rumbled into her thoughts. "Listen!"

"A motor!" Field exclaimed. "There's a boat coming, by Billings Spit." They watched the beam of light as the boat swung around the spit and into the basin.

"Shine your flashlight, Diggon, so they'll see us."

He aimed the flashlight at the boat, blinking it off and on. As it came closer, he said, "Isn't that your cabin cruiser?"

It was Dad all right, but Beth wouldn't relax her grip, not yet. When his boat drew up alongside, Field tossed him the rope. Without a word, he tied it to the stern of his boat and towed them closer to shore. "Row in from here," he said. "Your mother's waiting." He untied the rowboat, then went off to dock the cruiser.

When they reached the shore they stumbled out of the rowboat, flexing stiff fingers and cramped muscles. Mom helped pull up the boat. "We were so worried," she cried. "You kids have turned my hair grey."

"You're not mad?" Chelsea asked.

"Mad?" She gave Chelsea's shoulder a squeeze. "I'm livid. But we'll save that for later." She put her other arm around Beth and herded them up the trail. "Come on, Field," she called over her shoulder. "You too, Diggon. We've got a lot to say to you."

Chapter 26

The first thing Chelsea noticed was the verandah. Hundreds of cranes turned in the wind, rustling softly as muted chimes. Colours shimmered in the lamplight. "It looks like a festival! Especially with the lantern."

"Nice touch, don't you think?" her aunt said. "The wind knocked down a power line, so it's lanterns all the way."

"There's so many cranes! Way more than before! Did you — ?"

"Did I make them? Not likely, with my fumbly fingers. No, Beth made a whole bunch before you even arrived. She told me this morning I could string them up with the others, to surprise you. Looks great, doesn't it? Although I think we've run out of rafters."

"They're beautiful, Beth." Chelsea turned to her cousin, but Beth walked past without speaking.

Inside, the cabin smelled of warmth and

cinnamon and the fragrance of pine-scented oil burning in the lamps. Aunt Carolyn made them sit by the fire while she ladled out mugs of the hot apple cider simmering on top of the stove. "Eat up," she said, passing around a plate of sandwiches. "You must be famished. They're five hours old, but I'm sure that won't bother you."

As they dug into the sandwiches, she handed out sweaters and afghans. "Bundle up. You don't want to get a chill."

"Mom," Field said, pushing away the afghan, "it's boiling in here."

"So what's with the goose bumps?" She tucked it back around his legs. "And you, my boy, are in no position to argue."

They were halfway through the cider when Uncle Rob came in. "So," he said, eyeballing them one by one. There was a heavy silence. Cinnamon sticks clinked dully against the sides of the mugs. The fire snapped and crackled. Oil lamps spluttered in the stillness, shifting shadows on the walls. "Whose idea was it?"

Eyes glanced up from the steaming mugs, flitted from one face to another, then looked down. What idea is he talking about? Chelsea wondered. Going to the bay in the first place? Rowing back after dark? The ring of fire game, does he know about that already? A tiny heart pounded in her temple. "Mine," she said.

Unexpectedly, Diggon and Field joined in.

213

"Mine," they said, at the same time.

"Oh?" Uncle Rob looked surprised. "Well. Tomorrow morning we'll have a serious talk about this whole business. For now you can warm up, finish those sandwiches, and off to bed. There's a spare sleeping bag in Field's room, Diggon, and an air mattress. You're welcome to it."

"Thanks. I left my sleeping bag at the cove."

"We got a phone call this afternoon. Your parents are frantic. They'll be here Thursday morning to take you home."

"What? How did they — "

"How did they know you were here? Your parents know you better than you think. They knew you'd end up at the cove. And if you ended up there, you'd end up here, sooner or later." He placed another log on the fire, then ladled himself a mug of cider. "We've got news for you, Chelsea."

"Dad? Is he — "

"No, the news is from your mom. We got a message in a roundabout way. A letter was postmarked Singapore, mailed to you in care of your dad, and read to me over the phone by the doctor. She's heading home in a week or so and will be coming to collect you. And she's married. Simon Somebody. I guess you know him?"

Chelsea nodded and looked away, not trusting herself to speak. She folded her feelings tightly, marvelling at how quickly it all came back, how skilfully she could make herself small. The tightness pushed against her chest, in her throat, behind her eyes. She stared at the darkness beyond the window, longing to cry.

PART 6

BACK TO MY HOME,
I DARE NOT GO

Chapter 27

Beth sat at the table with the others and listened to the flutter of paper cranes. She knew the lecture was coming. She also knew it would be a long ordeal. Her father wouldn't be rushed.

She watched as he refilled her mom's coffee cup, finished his second piece of toast, methodically brushed the crumbs from his fingers, and started to clear away the breakfast dishes. "I can do that," she said, anxious to get moving.

"Stay." His tone left no room for argument.

Finally, after sitting down and pouring himself a cup of coffee, he was ready to begin. "I'm not going to elaborate on how worried we were," he said. "How we saw the rowboat at Diggon's and figured you were off hiking in the bush somewhere. Of course, when we found the shed door open and the motor gone, and saw the marks where the runabout had been dragged across the beach, we figured it out. What made us slightly furious was the fact that for all we knew, Diggon wasn't there. And you three — " he paused dramatically to eyeball Chelsea, Beth, and Field " — you three had somehow gotten into the shed. After we got the phone call, we realized Diggon was probably with you. Only problem was, where.

"I'm not going to dwell on how we searched every cove, every bay, every island in the basin. We never dreamed you'd be stupid enough, or irresponsible enough, to go outside the basin, not when you've been under strict orders not to. However, by suppertime, when you still hadn't shown up, we had to face the possibility that yes, you might have been that stupid and that irresponsible."

He stopped to pour himself another cup of coffee. Added some cream and two heaping spoonfuls of sugar and stirred. And stirred.

Get on with it, Beth wanted to shout. Even though she knew it was hopeless. That's how he dealt with problems at school: bored the kids out of their minds with talk, talk, talk. So calm, so rational. So infuriatingly reasonable. Get on with it! She wished Mom would take over. Mom was like Beth, outrage and outburst, fast, furious, and finished. Obviously, she'd decided to let Dad handle this one.

He took a sip of coffee and continued. "Now. Do you realize how many beaches and coves there are between here and the strait? Not to mention the river. Oh yes, we checked that too, past the bridge as far as the flats.

"Do you realize how rough it was out on the strait? Do you?" He paused and waited while they nodded. "How many times have I told you about that danger zone? Do you realize how close we came to calling the Coast Guard?" He took a deep breath and let it out slowly. "The important thing is, you're home and you're safe. At least you didn't try to get back by boat, at least not from the bay. That shows someone was thinking."

If he saw the sudden lifting of heads and furtive glances around the table, he pretended not to notice. "But rowing across the basin, at night, in that wind?" He shook his head and took another sip of coffee. "It's not only you two we were worried about," he said, looking at Beth and Field, "but Diggon. And Chelsea, of course. We're all responsible for Chelsea, as long as she's here." He directed his gaze to Chelsea, forcing her to look up. "As long as she's here, she's part of the family."

Beth heard the softening in his tone and wanted to scream. Responsible for Chelsea? Forget it! Wait till I tell you, Dad. She felt an explosion of words bursting to get out. Matches, fire, sick games, that's what Chelsea's all about. *Her*, part of the family? Never! "Dad, listen," she began. She was about to tell him everything when she caught the look on Chelsea's face. A fleeting look, gone in an instant, but filled with such crushing, unexpected sadness that Beth faltered and remained silent.

"What is it?" he asked.

"Nothing."

"So!" She jumped as her father banged his empty coffee cup on the table. "You're grounded, there's no two ways about that. And I mean grounded in the literal sense. On land. Off the water. No boats. In fact, Field — you're painting the rowboat. Sand it down first, inside and out, then give it three coats. There's paint and brushes in the boathouse. Diggon, until your parents get here, you follow the house rules. That means you help Field paint the boat. When that's done, you stack firewood."

Diggon cleared his throat. "What about — "

"Your boat? I'm towing it back this morning. Right now, as a matter of fact. As for you two," he said, turning to the girls, "you're picking blackberries. It's a bit early in the season so it'll take you a good long while. I want two buckets filled. Then you can whip up a pie. After that, you dig for clams. You're responsible for supper, and tonight we're living off the land. "

"But why do *we* have to . . . " Beth began.

Her father cut her off. "That's it." He got up from the table and walked down the steps and across the lawn.

"Wait, Dad." Field ran after him. "How long are we grounded?"

He turned and faced his son. "Fielding Robert Tennison, there's a time to ask questions and there's a time to remain silent. Learn to be a reader of those times."

"Wait! Does that mean we're — "

"That means the boat is where you left it. Check it out."

"Did you say three coats? Couldn't we — "

"Now!"

Chapter 28

It felt good, Diggon thought, scraping the sides of
the boat, sanding away the old chips of paint.
Rough edges smoothed out, smooth bits rough-
ened up so the new paint would hold. He tore off
a corner of sandpaper and put it in his pocket for
later, so he could sand his carving of the heron..

"Whew!" Field said repeatedly. "I thought
Dad would kill us."

"Really?"

"No, not really. He never gets that mad. He's
never even spanked us. We just discuss things,
calmly and rationally," he said, in a perfect imitation of his father. "What about your dad? Did you
ever get spanked?"

"My dad doesn't hit; he yells. If he's got time.
Which is practically never."

"Yeah, but he's coming to get you. Will he yell
then? What did you do, anyway?"

"Nothing." He said it automatically. *Nothing.*

The catch-all word to explain everything. Chelsea would probably have said the same thing. What are you doing with that tank of gas? Nothing.

"Oh," said Field.

Another automatic response. *What did you do? Nothing.*

Oh. End of story. But it wasn't, was it? "I did something I wasn't proud of," he heard himself saying. "Something I can't get out of my head."

Field's face shone with anticipation. Now it was coming, Diggon's secret that even Beth didn't know. "What?"

"I tried to be something I wasn't. Tried to fit in where I didn't belong."

"But what did you do?"

"I was hanging out with a bunch of guys after a party and I stood and watched while they beat up this kid. He hadn't done anything, he was just there, walking along the sidewalk, on his way home. And they grabbed him and — anyway, I didn't stop them. Didn't even try. Even when the kid was really hurt I didn't stop them. See what I mean? I did nothing."

"But — " Field felt cold, suddenly. He'd expected — what? Something daring and exciting, but not beating up on some innocent kid. Not that. Not Diggon standing there watching, letting it happen. The thought made him sick. "*You?* I don't get it." He stared hard at Diggon, trying to put the face of this other person onto the face he knew and trusted. But he couldn't. It just didn't fit. "So now what?"

"I'm going to face it."

"You're going to tell?" Stupid question. Diggon wouldn't do that, anymore than Field would tell on Chelsea.

"You got it."

"But those guys, what'll they do when you tell?"

"Figure it out."

"But Diggon . . ."

"Don't worry about it."

For a while the only sounds were the rasping of sandpaper, the crunch of feet on pebbles and broken shells, the screeching of gulls. What was happening to everybody? Field wondered. You have somebody all figured out, you think you know them, then *surprise!* Even Beth was different. Like with that ring of fire. Any other time she would have cheered to see him in that kind of fix. But no, suddenly she was playing the heroine, captain of the rescue squad or something. And rowing the boat in that wind when the tiniest whitecap gave her convulsions . . . It was too much. Far too much to think about on such a hot day. A swim, that's what he needed. As soon as this job was done.

He ran his hand along the edge of the boat. "I think it's ready for paint now." He picked up a can of marine enamel and handed it to Diggon.

"Can you get this lid off?"

"Sure." Diggon pried open the lid and stirred the red paint. "Got some brushes?"

"Tons." Field handed him one. "Do it fast, OK? Otherwise it's going to take forever."

Diggon dipped the brush into the paint and spread it over the surface of the boat. One stroke, and already it made a difference. He drew the brush along, liking the way the paint slid on, thick and glossy. Liking the smell of newness.

Beside him, Field started a stream of chatter, one minute complaining about the grounding, the next minute rejoicing over the blood-red fingerprints he'd be able to leave on everything. "And know what? Mom said we could have a bonfire tonight. I didn't expect that, did you? Not after last night. It's because my Uncle Mark, that's Chelsea's dad, is off the critical list. His memory's working good too, the doctor said. And it's because your parents are coming tomorrow and you'll be going back to Vancouver . . . "

Diggon hardly listened. Once in a while he put in a "really?" or "yeah," thankful that Field didn't seem to want anything more. It was a relief hearing the small voice talk about safe, everyday things. At least he wasn't going on and on about the other stuff, asking questions, wanting all the gory details. Surprising, actually, knowing Field. It was as if he didn't believe it. Or didn't want to believe it. So he simply moved on to other things.

If only I could, Diggon thought, as he quietly layered on the paint.

It was a sturdy, well-built rowboat. Made it all the way across the basin without getting swamped. Amazing. Even more amazing was the fact that his parents were coming — on a weekday — to take him home. They would actually miss work. Unheard of! Even when he was sick Mom would just nip home for an hour or so, check to see what state he was in, or if he was still alive. If he was, so long, get some sleep, catch you later.

What state would they be in when they got here?

He dipped the brush in the paint, swirled it around, and lifted it out, not caring that it dripped red blotches all over his running shoes. As the brush swept along the edge of the boat he realized he didn't care what state his parents were in. The fact that they were coming was enough.

That's the easy part, the voice needled. *Your parents are nothing compared to the rest.*

Doesn't matter, Diggon answered. Even though his stomach churned at the thought of going to the cops.

The cops? Even that's not the worst part.

I know, I know. He felt a sharp pain, as if splinters of wood were digging into his chest. He had to take what was coming. Then, no matter what they did to him, the voice would be silenced.

You think so? What about the kid? You think you can make it right for him?

No.

It stunned him, the horrifying reality that no, he could never make it right. But he could play the last danger game, facing what he feared the most. And somehow get back to being himself.

"Hey, Diggon, wake up. You've got paint running down your arm." Field picked up the paint can. "Come on, it's time to do the other side."

Later, during a brief moment when Field had stopped talking, they heard the blast of a horn. Diggon looked up quickly, thinking it might be his parents. But it wasn't. "Whose car's that?" he wondered.

Field looked across the meadow and caught a glimpse of a black Corvette winding through the trees towards the cabin. "Beats me." He shrugged and went back to his painting.

Chapter 29

The best blackberries grew at the edge of the road leading down to Billings Spit. Even if it was early in the season, a lot of berries were ripe-ready for picking and tumbled into their hands at the slightest touch. Chelsea tasted one, juicy and sweet. Then helped herself to more.

"Don't stand there eating," Beth snapped.

Chelsea looked up, surprised. Not by the tone of Beth's voice, but by the fact she was speaking to her at all.

The walk to the spit had not been pleasant. Beth had set an impossible pace, expecting Chelsea to follow. But no matter how quickly Chelsea walked she couldn't catch up. Finally, disappointed, she gave up trying.

She had felt a strong urge to talk about her father. She wanted to tell Beth how great he'd sounded on the phone that morning. He was looking at several weeks of physiotherapy for his fractured leg, but by October he expected to be close to normal. "No Ironman Triathlon though," he'd said. "Not this year."

"Gee Dad, it breaks my heart. But you hate running anyway."

"Why do you think I broke my leg?" he joked.

After hanging up, she realized how much she wanted to be with him again. It was almost enough to make her forget the news about her mother.

From behind, Chelsea had read Beth's anger in the set of her shoulders, the way she held her head. She had wanted to thank Beth for the cranes, but it clearly wasn't the time.

After Uncle Rob's talk, Beth had stomped into the cabin, grabbed the buckets from Aunt Carolyn, and literally thrown one at Chelsea.

"Beth!" Aunt Carolyn had scolded. "That's no way to —"

"Sorry." Beth glowered at Chelsea and stormed out the door.

She hadn't spoken another word until now. "Well, come on. Start picking." She pushed past Chelsea and trampled down the bushes, making a path so she could reach the berries farther in. "The best ones are always the hardest to get," she grumbled.

"If you say so." Chelsea followed her example and trampled down her own path. "I've never picked blackberries before."

"Seriously?" Beth was so surprised she forgot

to sound angry. "No roasted marshmallows, no blackberries. You're totally depraved. Sorry, I mean deprived." Or did she? Maybe depraved was the word to describe Chelsea. Depraved, perverted, weird, crazy . . . Through the tangle of blackberry leaves she caught a glimpse of Chelsea's face and saw that look again. Sad, troubled . . . Well, so what! Who didn't feel that way sometimes? She felt another surge of anger but let it go. It was too hot to feel angry. Too hot to feel anything but hot. And tired. She'd have it out with Chelsea some other time. Now, she didn't have the energy.

Brambles pricked fingers, added more scratches to bare legs, and snared loose strands of hair. Except for curses and exaggerated outbursts of pain, they picked without speaking, Beth in the sunshine, Chelsea in the shade.

"I'd say that was the last berry." Carefully Beth backed out of the bushes.

"No way," said Chelsea. "Look how full my bucket is compared to yours. You've got room for at least twenty more."

Beth stopped and looked at her cousin. That brief exchange of words was almost like a normal conversation. Almost pleasant. "Twenty? Get real. Maybe ten."

They picked a few more, then headed back along the beach. A light breeze ruffled the water, and seagulls wheeled overhead. Chelsea squealed suddenly as a cold spray of water shot up her leg. "What was that?"

Beth laughed. "It's only a clam. See those holes? That's where the clams are. That's where we'll be digging later. See? If you look across the beach you can see a whole bunch of squirts. Like little fountains."

"Beth, I'm sorry about yesterday. You know, about the fire. And Field. There wasn't any danger. The flames die down after a while . . . " Her voice trailed off. She felt Beth bristle and wished she hadn't brought up the subject. But it had to be said. "And I'm sorry about Diggon. It's not what you think."

Beth watched a kingfisher hover on rapidly beating wings, then plunge headlong into the water. "Maybe not," she said. "Maybe I did jump to the wrong conclusion, about you and Diggon, I mean. That fire stuff, though, that's — I don't know. Maybe you should — Oh, forget it. I know I jump to conclusions. I'm always doing that. Then I end up with both feet in my mouth, looking like a jerk."

Chelsea nodded. "You are pretty funny looking."

"Get out!" Beth laughed and nudged her with an elbow.

Chelsea nudged back. "Remember that time I asked if you had a boyfriend — "

"When you wouldn't tell me if *you* did — "

" — and you said, sort of. It was Diggon you

meant, wasn't it?"

"No way."

"Anybody with two eyes can see it."

"Then why did you — "

"I told you, it wasn't like that. If you hadn't rushed off, I would have explained."

Beth thought for a moment. "Is it really that obvious? I mean about Diggon."

"Totally obvious."

She sighed. "I try so hard to be cool."

Chelsea burst out laughing. "You, cool? Try a hot lava sandwich."

"Whoa! That cool, huh?"

"Yes, that cool!"

"How about pepperoni? No? Not that cool, either?"

Chelsea slapped her on the back. "Come on! Race you back!"

Still laughing, they ran across the beach, over rocks and barnacles and slippery pools of seaweed, stopping only when they reached the boathouse.

"Whew!" Chelsea gasped. "Talk about cool!"

"Would you stop it! My stomach hurts from laughing." She leaned against the boathouse, relieved that some of the tension had gone away. "Doesn't the rowboat look great? I can't believe those two did such a good job. I hope Dad recorded the moment."

"They did a good job of painting the beach, too," Chelsea said, stepping over the puddles of red paint.

"At least they put everything away. Field usually leaves a big mess for someone else to clean up."

"The boat looks different."

Beth agreed. "I'm glad they painted it. Now I can go rowing and not think terrified, terrified."

"I was scared, too," Chelsea admitted.

"You were?"

"Not panic scared, more like excited scared. I like outside dangers. They're not as bad as the inside ones."

Outside, inside, what was she talking about? Beth wondered. What did she mean, "inside dangers"? She was about to ask when she spotted the car, parked in the trees beside the cabin. "Someone's here."

Chelsea looked up and froze. Her cheeks, flushed from the running and the sun, turned white.

"Hey, Chelsea. What's the matter?"

"Nothing." She handed Beth her bucket. "Will you take this for me? I want to stay on the beach for a while."

She watched Beth walk across the meadow, swinging the buckets, not a care in the world. Across the lawn, up the steps, and onto the verandah where a group of people sat around the table. Her aunt and uncle, Field and Diggon, and two newcomers.

Her mother. And Simon.

Chapter 30

Some things, Chelsea thought, are definites. Like the paint on the boat, definitely wet. Like the tide, definitely coming in. Like the container of paint thinner, definitely not put away. And me, she thought, picking up the paint thinner, definitely not going back.

There. A decision. How simple it was, making that decision. Simple Simon. So why didn't she feel relieved? Why did she still feel that tightness inside?

She sat with her back against the boathouse, knees bent almost to her chin. The paint thinner sloshed against the sides of the container as she set it down, reminding her of the waves splashing against the boat. Was it only last night? She wished the boat had been swamped. Everyone would have been rescued, of course, except for her. She would have drifted away, down, down, and away, her hair streaming like seaweed.

Unconsciously, her fingers curled around the matchbox in her pocket. Her hand drew it out. Time for this again? Oh, yes.

Did you ever see a flame, burn away the pain?

Field's song played in her head.

Down by the Bay, where the watermelons grow
Back to my home, I dare not go
For if I do, my mother will say
Did you ever —

No mother, I never.

Never could look the way you wanted.

Never could be what you wanted.

Invisible.

Sorry I couldn't erase myself. Sorry I couldn't vanish. Tried awfully hard though, remember? Running away, hiding in closets, crouching in dark corners where I wouldn't be seen.

Did you ever see Chelsea, a nine-year-old ghost in a white cotton sheet the night of the Halloween party, the night — Stop. That doesn't rhyme and the rhythm's all wrong.

More than the rhythm was wrong, that night.

Did you ever see Chelsea, hiding from her mommy?

Yes, and we know who found you. *This will be our little secret. Isn't this fun? Your ghost sheet is big enough for both of us to hide under.*

Stop it.

It's a game! Simon says, touch your mouth. Simon says, touch my mouth. Simon says, touch my knee. Simon says, touch my —

Don't. I don't like this.

Come on, it doesn't hurt, does it? Just a little tickle. There. Now it's your turn. Our little secret. And you will never tell.

But I told. *Mommy, he —*

Don't you ever tell such stories again. He's daddy's friend, a family friend. How could you! To say such things when he's been so good to you. I never want to hear talk like that again, do you hear me?

Simon. Struck out with a match.

Did you ever —

No mother, I never told again. Not after you hit me for lying. But I learned how to get rid of Simon, every time. I cut him out of paper and burned him up, head, shoulders, knees, and toes, like the kindergarten song. Only sometimes I started with the toes. I liked watching the paper curl and blacken till there was nothing left. Till he was undone.

Did you ever —

Yes, I burned other things. Sometimes your letters. I liked seeing the ashes, knowing that some connection to your life was gone. Sometimes I burned Simon's letters. Not many, not often. I was careful. You never knew, but I knew. Every time Simon touched me — yes, *there* — every time I heard his footsteps in the hall, the door opening, his voice whispering *Simon says . . . show and tell* — every time, I could unfold that little bit of knowledge and feel strong.

Did you ever —

No, I never liked Simon. Maybe at first, but after? No. Simon is scum. I hated him, hated his presents, hated him.

Happy Birthday, Chelsea. Eleven years old and such a charmer . . . Let's see how much you've grown. Come on, show and tell . . . No sweetheart, I'm not talking about your height . . .

Stop it.

That didn't hurt, did it? Simon says, touch my . . .

NO

Come on, show and touch . . .

STOP IT! I'M GOING TO TELL!

But look what happened the last time you told. Your daddy moved away. And your mother was so angry at you for lying, remember? Do you want to upset her again? She might not want you. She might send you away. Come on, now. We care about each other, don't we? And people who like each other as much as we do want to feel good.

But I don't like you. I hate you and I'll burn you up and spit on your ashes and trample them into the dirt and you'll be gone, like these words screaming into the pillow . . .

When the small fires weren't enough, I made them bigger. Like the fire in the lane. And the fire at school, the one in the washroom I got suspended for. Remember, Mom, the last straw? I wanted you to take notice and say, Chelsea, I love you, it'll be different from now on, just you and me, and maybe Dad will come back. And I wanted to hurt you, so you'd wake up shuddering in the middle of the night, wondering when I'd strike the next match. And where.

So much for good intentions. That fire gave you the perfect excuse to throw me out.

Did you ever —

Yes, mother, I loved you. But I could never do it right. I wanted to. I tried. And now you've come back. With Simon. Knowing what I know you know.

Did you ever see Chelsea pour the paint thinner —

Terrible rhyme. Not to mention the rhythm.

— and strike the match?

Will you notice me then, Mom? Will you?

Chapter 31

Beth was impressed with Alison, her exotic aunt with the fascinating past. Except for the physical resemblance, it was hard to imagine her as Chelsea's mother. Hard to imagine her as a mother, period. Had she actually changed diapers? Impossible.

But as an aunt, she was sublime. Unbelievably cool. And gorgeous. She wore a fuchsia-coloured dress, clinched at the waist by a belt of turquoise stones interwoven with rings of silver. Her hair tumbled over her shoulders like Chelsea's, although it was shorter and lighter. Her eyes were like Chelsea's too, only not so intense. She caught Beth staring at her and smiled, as if she were used to such scrutiny and didn't mind it one bit.

As for Simon, he was gorgeous too, Beth had to admit. A real hunk. And totally relaxed, leaning back in his chair, looking quite at home. "How nice to meet you," he'd said warmly, when they were introduced. He stood up and shook her hand, ignoring the blackberry stains on her fingers. He even complimented her on the paper cranes.

"It was Chelsea, mostly," Beth said. "I'm not very good at it."

"You must visit the gallery next fall. All of you. An origami artist is coming from Japan, the best in the world. He does incredible work, origami the size of your fingernail. Really!" he smiled.

Beth smiled back. She'd love to go to Vancouver and visit his gallery.

As well as being gorgeous, Aunt Alison was a natural storyteller with an expressive voice and gestures to match. Her face shone with excitement as she told of catching dragonflies in Bali and roasting them for a snack, parasailing in the Gulf of Siam, riding elephants in Northern Thailand, sneaking across the border into Burma under cover of darkness, escaping the patrols by "this much."

"Why did you go there?" Field asked.

She leaned forward and patted his paint-smeared cheek. "For the adventure," she said, in her lilting English accent.

Diggon, like Field, seemed mesmerized by her tales. Even Mom and Dad were listening, enthralled, although now and then Beth caught them exchanging glances. The kind she'd learned to describe as "meaningful," whatever that meant.

Alison had brought a backpack filled with

trinkets and treasures. "There you go," she said. There was a clattering, rustling, and tinkling as she dumped everything onto the table. "Take your pick. You too, Diggon." Everything from wooden elephant clappers and carvings of Balinese gods to dangly silver earrings and hand-painted scarves of Thai silk.

Beth picked up a scarf blazing with red and orange hibiscus. "This would look perfect on Chelsea."

"Absolutely!" Alison agreed. "Perfect with her hair and colouring."

"Where is she, anyway?" Simon asked. "Lost in the blackberries? Or is she building a sand sculpture? She was always a great one for that."

"It's not a sandy beach," said Field.

"So much for that, then." Simon glanced at his Rolex. "No big rush, Ali, but don't forget we do have a ferry to catch."

"I'm sure she's not far," said Alison. "Strolling on the beach, chatting to clams, no doubt. She is a bit of a strange one. Probably doesn't even know we're here. I hope she hasn't been a bother. Has she been all right?"

"Good of you to ask," Mom said. Rather curtly, Beth thought, for Mom. Surely this wasn't the first time Alison had wondered about Chelsea. After all, they'd been here at least an hour.

"I'll take a look down the beach," said Simon. "See if I can hustle her up."

"That's OK, I'll go," Diggon said. "Have to check on the boat anyway, see if the paint's dry." He brushed past Simon and started down the stairs.

Beth watched him, surprised. What was the hurry? Since when did he care if the paint was dry, especially with his Coke left unfinished? Racing off to see Chelsea, that's what this was all about. *It's not what you think*, she had said. Sure, Chelsea. And to think I actually believed you.

She made a quick decision. "Wait, Diggon!" Then grabbed the scarf and ran after him.

"Do the second coat, OK, Beth?" Field called.

"In your dreams," she muttered.

"What?" Diggon stopped and waited for her to catch up.

"Nothing."

He glanced at the scarf. "You go ahead if you like, give that to Chelsea. Tell her . . . well, you know."

"Her mom's here and Simon's here. She already knows. She saw the car."

"She didn't say anything? About . . . " He hesitated and looked towards the verandah. "About Simon?"

"No!" Beth laughed. "Why should she?"

Diggon looked as though he were about to say something, then changed his mind. "You go talk to her then. I'll stay up here."

"OK, sure," she said.

She spotted Chelsea sitting against the far side of the boathouse, gazing at the water with a fixed, almost prayerful expression on her face. She crept closer and crouched behind a tall stand of grasses, not wanting to intrude.

Chelsea took a match from the box in her hand and lit it. Before the flame reached her fingers, she blew it out softly, her breath like a blessing. She lit another match, then another. Beth stared, afraid to move, afraid of what Chelsea might do if she knew she was being watched, or if she was taken by surprise. Each time she blew out the flame, she placed the charred matchstick on the ground. A pattern seemed to be emerging. A circle of burnt offerings? Letters, spelling out a message? What game was she playing now?

She leaned over, rearranged a couple of matches, and whispered something Beth couldn't hear. Then she wiped the bits of charcoal from her fingers, picked up the container beside her, and unscrewed the lid.

Beth gasped. Even from a distance, the fumes were unmistakable. Horrified, she watched as Chelsea lifted the container, raised it to her shoulders, tipped it so that the liquid —

"No!" With one long scream she raced over and knocked the container out of Chelsea's hands. "What are you doing? You — "

"Nothing! I'm just — "

"What did you think was in here, water?" Beth

grabbed the container and twisted the lid back on. "This is paint thinner! It's highly flammable, don't you know that? What're you doing out here with paint thinner and matches? Wasn't your ring of fire game enough? Give me those." She pried the matches from Chelsea's hand. "God, Chelsea, are you crazy?"

She moved the container well out of reach and sat down, her chest heaving, her breath coming in painful gasps. "I don't believe this. Of all the stupid — What were you planning to do, set yourself on fire? It wasn't enough to terrorize my brother, you have to set yourself — What's the matter with you?" She turned to the burnt matchsticks, carefully arranged to form the word PELE. "Oh, I get it. Pele, the fire goddess. Like when you saw her walking across the lava and it was supposed to mean something? You think *this* was it? The big meaning? That's crap, Chelsea."

She picked up a handful of stones and tossed them at a log, listening to the thwack, thwack, waiting to calm down. Why do I bother? she wondered. Why don't I just let her do what she wants? There she sits, steady as ever, while I'm the one that's losing it. Talk about depraved. Finally, she turned to Chelsea. "Why?"

Chelsea continued to stare straight ahead, her face taut. "I'm not going back."

"Back where? What are you talking about?"

"*Back to my home, I dare not go.* Like in the

song. You know when we were at the bay and you said you had a new danger game, telling secrets?"

"Yeah," Beth said. She felt calmer now, ready to listen to whatever Chelsea decided to tell her. She'd be leaving soon anyway. Aunt Alison and Simon would take her home. "Sorry I bugged you about it, your secret or whatever. Maybe we should — "

"I do have a secret. It's a game, and I've had to play since I was, since I . . ." She broke down, her voice choking with tears. When she spoke again, the words came in a rush. "It was show and tell Simon, and Simon Says, and I had to, and he'd come to my room at night when Mom was out or after school in the lane and I had to, and I tried to say no and I tried to tell, but my mother . . . and the whole time . . ." She gave an agonizing cry. Tears streamed down her face, her body shook with sobs. "And the whole time, *she knew!*"

Something opened inside Beth, an understanding so huge, so frightening, so devastating, for a moment she didn't know what to do. For a moment it was as though everything had stopped except for this terrible knowledge drumming inside her head, tearing at her heart.

And then, not knowing what else to do, she opened her arms to Chelsea and held her while she cried.

"Here," Beth said, finally handing Chelsea the

scarf. "Your mom brought this back from Thailand. Especially for you."

"I know she didn't," said Chelsea, "but thanks." She wiped her face with the flaming hibiscus, then blew her nose.

"Chelsea, that's a silk scarf!"

"I don't have anything else. Do you? It'll wash." She crumpled it into a soggy ball and stuffed it in her pocket.

"What are you going to do now?"

Chelsea gave her a blank look.

"Your mom's up at the cabin with Simon and he wants to get going. So what are you going to do?"

"I'm not going back."

"So don't," Beth said. "Stay here with us. But whatever you do, you've got to tell."

Tell. The four-letter word pounded in Chelsea's head.

"Tell again and again until someone believes you. I believe you, Mom'll believe you, and she'll know what to do. OK? You've got to."

Chelsea nodded. "Thanks."

"For what?"

"For listening. For being a friend. You're good at that."

For a long time they sat without speaking, watching the incoming tide. When Beth did speak, she picked her way cautiously over the words as if she were crossing a stream on stepping stones, in danger of falling in. "The paint thinner. The matches. All that stuff with fire. If I hadn't been here . . . Were you . . . ?"

The question mark hung between them. Finally, Chelsea said, "But you were. And I didn't."

Chapter 32

"Chelsea!" Her mother walked lightly along the path, hurrying to meet the girls as they came up from the beach. "It's so good to see you."

"Mom, I need to talk to you. Now. On the beach."

"Can't it wait? Simon's chomping at the bit. We really ought to — "

"I'll tell him you'll be right back," said Beth. She gave Chelsea a nod of encouragement and ran towards the cabin.

"You don't look too bad, considering," Mom said as she followed Chelsea across the bridge. "Except for the paint on your shorts. What have you been sitting in? The boys are covered in red paint, too. You all need a good splash of turpentine."

She bent down to remove a pebble from her sandal. "Your father's coming along, I take it. I certainly was surprised to get that telegram. An accident of all things, when you'd only been there — what was it — a couple of weeks?"

"Just over three." She steered her mother towards the boathouse.

"We would've come back sooner but I didn't get the telegram until we arrived in Bangkok. That was the only mailing address I'd left, you see." She sat on a log and stretched out her long tanned legs. "Not the best beach for walking on, is it? Not like Thailand. Oh, the beaches. Stunning! I'm rather sorry we had to rush home, still . . . there's always next time. Perhaps we'll take you with us, would you like that? You know, I think things will be a lot better from now on. More settled. You've had time to get rid of all that anger, and if you need someone, like a counsellor — you know, for that fire business — well, it can be arranged. Whatever you like. And I do think you're better off with me than with your father. If it hadn't been that accident it would have been another one." She gave a dry laugh. "That's Mark."

Chelsea picked up a box half-hidden amongst the broken shells.

"I've been doing a lot of thinking," Mom continued. "I admit I haven't been the best of mothers, but still . . . Perhaps we could be friends. I'd like that, Chelsea. Really. And Simon — "

"You shouldn't have, Mom. Not Simon." Her voice was cold.

"What on earth do you mean?" She glanced up quickly. "You know how I love Simon, always have, even before your father and I were divorced. We've always been the best of friends. And he's been so good to you."

"You shouldn't have. Because I'm going to tell."

Her mother raised a hand, shielding her eyes from the glare of the sun. "I'm not sure I understand."

Chelsea's legs trembled. She felt the familiar strangling in her throat. For an instant, she faltered.

"No!" she said suddenly. The force of the word surprised her. "You're not going to stop me. Not this time. I'm going to tell until something is done. Diggon and Beth believed me. Aunt Carolyn will believe me, so will Uncle Rob. And Dad. Yes!" The words exploded in her mother's face. "*Simon Says*, remember? Show and *touch!*"

There. The words were out and there was no turning back. "I'm going to tell when and where and what and how long and I'm going to end it. You knew!" she cried. "You knew about Simon. And you let it happen!"

With shaking fingers she opened the box Beth had left lying on the beach. She took out a match, struck it, and held it between them. "See?" She swallowed hard. "One minute you have something. The next minute — " She blew out the flame. "The next minute, you don't. Extinguished, Mom. That's what you did to me."

Chapter 33

It was a quiet bonfire. No one felt much like talking, let alone singing, although Field did his best to liven things up.

"Give it a rest," Beth said. "We're sick of *Down by the Bay*, period. Try disappearing."

"Why don't you?"

When the fire died down, they steamed clams over the coals and ate them straight from the shells with twists of lemon. "You want some garlic?" Field handed Beth the shaker of garlic salt. "Sprinkle it on your clams. It's good."

"Gross, you mean. Yuck."

For dessert they had thick slices of blackberry pie. "Are you sure you don't want any more, Chelsea? You picked the berries."

"No thanks, Uncle Rob. I'm not that hungry."

"Try it with marshmallow." Field showed them how he'd roasted marshmallows and smeared the melted mess all over his pie. "It's great!"

"It's disgusting," Beth said. "Take it away, would you? We're not impressed."

"Too bad Aunt Alison and Simon couldn't stay," he went on, licking blackberry juice from his paint-stained fingers. "They would've liked this, don't you think? How come they left so soon?"

No one answered.

"Do you think they really ate dragonflies? That's what I call gross. Hey, Chelsea, if you don't want another piece of pie, can I have it? Chelsea?"

"What? Oh, sure. Help yourself."

He did.

Dad picked up the video camera. "How about one last shot, while Diggon's here. I'll call this episode *Reflections*. What do you think, Beth?"

"Yeah, Dad!" said Field. "Get my pie invention and call it *Complexions*. Isn't that what you call desserts and stuff?"

Beth rolled her eyes. "No, that's *confections*. And you're a *defection* and that's what you're supposed to do. Like, defect. Get lost."

"Well, Beth? How about it?"

"Dad, why don't you leave it? For once."

He looked at her serious face, then turned to Diggon and Chelsea, both staring at the fire, lost in their own thoughts. "You're right," he said. "Another time." He packed the camera inside the case. "It's been a long day. A long two days, really. I'm heading up. Coming, Carolyn? You kids can stay here for a while."

"You mean I can stay, too?" said Field. "All right!" Not that there was much to stay for. The others sat spellbound, gazing at the fire as if they'd been drawn inside some kind of magic circle. Oh well. At least he could finish the marshmallows. And maybe Diggon wouldn't want the rest of his pie.

After a while, Chelsea surprised him by saying, "Come on, Field. Let's go down to the wharf, kick up some phosphorescence."

"Cool!" he exclaimed. He leaped to his feet, then stopped. "Are you — " He paused, frowning.

"Just the phosphorescence," she said. "Promise."

"OK then." He grabbed the flashlight and ushered her along the beach. "It's like fire in water, you know? I'll show you a good place to see it."

"And I'll tell you something," Chelsea said. "Remember that campfire song? Well, I'm going to tell you all about the gloaming . . ."

Beth listened to their fading voices. "He's in for a big disappointment."

"Maybe not," Diggon said. "Chelsea has a way of telling stories. Like those raven stories, and all that stuff about Pele, remember?"

Beth didn't answer. The last thing she wanted to do was talk about Chelsea.

For a long time they stared at the fire, weaving their own thoughts. "Your parents are coming tomorrow?" she said finally, knowing they were.

"Yeah."

"I hope, well, I hope everything will be OK. Whatever."

"Hard to say."

"Do you want to, I mean — "

"Talk about what happened? I don't know." Earlier, while the others were setting up on the beach, he had slipped away and phoned his parents. He told them everything. Then asked the question he had been dreading. "Is the kid all right? Have you heard anything, in the news, I mean?" His heart pounded in his ears. Somehow, he heard his father saying, "He's got a long, rough road ahead of him, but eventually he'll be fine."

Diggon swallowed hard. "I'm going to the cops, Dad. I've got to tell them what happened."

There was a slight pause. Then his father, in an unusually husky voice said, "I'm with you. Whatever happens, I'm there."

"Hey, Diggon?" Beth's voice drew him back. "Are you OK?"

"Yeah. Sorry, Beth. I can't talk about it. Not now."

She let out a deep breath, relieved. Chelsea's disclosure had been enough of a shock. She didn't think she could handle another one. "Yeah, well . . . I'm glad you came back. Even if it wasn't . . . well, you know."

"Me too. Look, I'm sorry about the letters. Things started happening." He shrugged. "I'm no good at writing letters, anyway."

"Yeah, well . . . Me neither. I mean — " What a conversation. Had she totally lost it? *Yeah. Well. I mean.* Hopeless. Try something else, Beth. "Do you think you'll be back? This summer, I mean? It's not over yet."

"I don't know. Maybe."

He moved closer and took something out of his pocket. "Found this in my hideout. You know that tunnel I made in the broom? I dug a hole in there a long time ago, to bury stuff. Like buried treasure, you know? I thought — well, here." He opened his hand.

"The arrowhead!" Beth smiled, her eyes shining. "I've been looking for one of these my whole life. Thanks, Diggon. But are you sure? I mean — "

He leaned over and kissed her. This time, their noses didn't get in the way.

Uncle Rob found Chelsea alone by the fire, long after the others had gone to bed. He picked up a stick and began poking at the coals, breaking them apart, pushing the embers together. "Your dad used to do this whenever we had a fire. Used to drive our parents crazy, the way he couldn't leave it alone. He liked watching things flare up. He'd get into such fights with our dad. Once a year he'd run away from home."

Chelsea looked up, surprised. "He did?"

"Starting from his first day in kindergarten. 'I hate it,' he said. Loaded his wagon and took off down the street. It was raining, so he only went a couple of blocks. But each year he went a bit farther."

The image of her dad as a five-year-old run-away made Chelsea smile. He'd never told her that story. Not many other ones, either. Soon, hopefully, there would be time. "Were you — " She paused. "Did you like each other?"

"Sure, I liked my brother. But we never spent that much time together. Except for summers, here at Tidewater. Then we got pretty close. No one else around, I guess. To tell you the truth, I never felt he liked me all that much. Probably thought I was too conservative and boring." He chuckled. "He was probably right."

"But he must like you. Otherwise, why would he want me to stay with you?"

"Good point, Chelsea. And I have to tell you, I'm glad he felt that way."

She smiled. "Me too."

"Talking about Mark reminds me of something he used to do when he was little, whenever we had beach fires here." He shook his head, smiling. "Funny that should come back to me, now."

"What did he do?"

"Floating wishes, he used to call it. He'd take a piece of driftwood, like this, then take a birthday candle, or the stub of a kitchen candle, like this . . ." He dug around in his pocket, brought out a can-dle, and held it to the fire. "Then he'd light the wick and drip the wax onto the wood. When there was a little pool of wax he'd stick the candle into it, like this." He held the candle in the melted wax until it hardened and the candle stood up straight, on its own.

"Now for the next step." He blew out the candle and walked towards the shore. "Coming?" he called over his shoulder.

Chelsea got up and followed.

When they were standing at the water's edge, he once again fumbled in his pocket. "Darnit," he said. "Here we are, all ready to go, and I forgot the matches. Chelsea, have you — "

"Here." She took the box from her pocket and handed it to him.

Taking a match, he struck it and lit the candle. "The idea is, you make a wish and set the wood on the water. The current will carry it away. If the candle goes out, you've lost it. But if it keeps burning, your wish will come true. Here, you do it."

She wanted to believe it. Silently, she made her wish. Then bent down and placed the wood on the water. For a long time she stood on the shore, watching her wish float away with the tide, the candle flame a small brightness flickering in the night.

"You know that we have to tell the police."

Chelsea nodded.

"You'll be fine, Chelsea," her uncle said, pocketing the matches. "You'll be fine."

PART 7

FIRES BURNING

Chapter 34

It was a perfect morning. Sky like a blue china plate, surf crashing against the rocks, black sand glistening, white foam sparkling. It's all here, Chelsea thought. Land, sea, and sky. And fire.

She smiled at her dad. This was the most walking he'd done since the accident, over four months ago. As soon as he was out of the hospital she'd flown back to Hawaii, just in time to start the new school year.

She took the water bottle from her pack and handed it to her dad, then sat beside him on the edge of the cliff and watched.

They had risen early from their new home in Naalehu, driven to Volcanoes National Park, then followed the road to where the new lava flow cut it off. From there they had hiked across the old lava field, Chelsea slowing down to match her father's pace, until they got as far as they could go.

Two weeks earlier Kilauea had erupted again, this time from a vent on the east rift zone. Two weeks later, lava was still flowing down the mountainside to the sea. Acres of rainforest were gone. Palm trees, gone. Fields, gone. Roads, gone. Chelsea's black sand beach, gone. Farther along the coast, Kawena's small community, gone. But wonder of wonders, their house was still there.

Dad took another long drink of water. "Everyone said I was crazy, buying that place. You're sitting on a time bomb, they said. Well, Chelsea, you win some, you lose some. I decided to take a chance. And look at it!" He shook his head, amazed. "It's still standing!"

For some inexplicable reason the flow had split, then come together, creating a small island untouched by lava. And in that island, still sheltered by palm trees, stood the house. Surrounded by fire, impossible to reach, but safe.

"You know what Kawena's going to say," Dad said.

"You mean when I saw that strange woman and gave her back her dog?"

He nodded. "She'll say you saw Pele, and since you were kind to her, something good has come of it."

Chelsea grinned. "I'd say she's right."

An explosion of steam drew their eyes away from the house. Lava was boiling up through cracks in the surface, pouring down the sides of rocks, and bubbling into the sea, forming new land. Even as the lava was destroying one beach, it was building another.

So much building, Chelsea thought. Something lost, but something gained. Would it work for her? Maybe one day she could approach her mother and say, *Tell me, I want to understand. I want to trust you.* But could she? Could she put their old relationship behind her and build a new one? Maybe. Maybe not.

She thought back to the day at Tidewater when she had forced her mother to listen. She remembered Mom's initial reaction — shock, disbelief, anger. But the question still remained. Was that anger directed at Simon? Or at her?

Then there was the hurt. Mom's face had crumpled before her eyes. She had suddenly grown small, sitting there with her knees drawn up, her arms clasped around her chest, rocking back and forth and back and forth, the soft tinkle of her earrings sounding empty and pathetic.

Had Mom known all along? Or did she honestly believe Chelsea had lied all those years ago? She had denied it that day on the beach at Tidewater. "I didn't know, I had no idea . . ."

But how could she *not* have known, and if she *had* known, how could she have let it happen? The questions burned in Chelsea's mind, turning over and over, layer after layer, but she never got to the core. Never got closer to understanding.

Maybe she never would. At least, not unless Mom told the truth. But what was the truth? Layer after layer, burning away.

And Simon. She shuddered. Even now, she felt the urge to strike the match. To take control.

There was another way. Aunt Carolyn had said, "The more you can talk about it, the more control you'll have."

She had gone with her aunt to the police and made a statement. The police told her they would lay charges. That there would be a trial — unless Simon confessed. But that wasn't likely. She knew she would have to testify in court. But could she go through with it? "Whatever happens," her aunt had said, "you have my support. Trust me." Beth had said the same. So had Uncle Rob.

But waiting for a trial could take months. Then what? She'd have to live it all over again. Could she?

Testifying would get it out in the open. She would be able to stand up and say, *This is me, Chelsea, and this is what happened and it wasn't my fault* . . .

"Your dad loves you," Uncle Rob had said. "He'll understand. And if he's well enough to travel I know he'll be with you for the trial. Don't be afraid to tell him."

But she was afraid. She kept hearing her mother's words from so long ago. *Don't you ever tell Daddy.* She'd tried to get them out of her head.

But what if he didn't believe her? What if she'd left it too late? Worse, what if he blamed her?

"Well, Chelsea?" His voice broke into her thoughts. "What do you think?" He gestured to the lava flow.

Red-orange streams, explosions of steam. Fiery spatters shot into the air and fell back into the sea. Waves rolled in, folding over, crashing against old cliffs and new land. She shook her head, unable to find the words.

"I know," he said. "I feel the same way."

All around the house, fires were burning. All around her, too. Within her, without her.

> *Fire's burning, fire's burning*
> *Draw nearer, draw nearer*
> *In the gloaming, in the gloaming*
> *Come sing and be merry.*

Maybe this is the way it has to be, she thought. Something lost, but something gained. Maybe it's not always sing and be merry. But that part, too, will come around.

The house was safe. And Dad was safe. Maybe she could be too. Maybe she could put out the fires, at least the ones burning inside.

She stared across the lava, wondering how to begin — where to begin. With Simon? With her mother? With the matches? Or with that long-ago November day, so different from this one, that Remembrance Day of origami cranes . . .

A flickering, bright against the blackness of

the lava, caught her eye. A figure emerged. Was it a trick of the light? Or was it Pele?

The figure floated across the steaming lava, long hair rippling in folds. Wherever her feet touched, small fires flared up. Through clouds of steam Chelsea watched as Pele shimmered in the distance. Farther away and farther, until with one final shimmer, she was gone. As if someone or something, with one light breath, had blown out the flame.

Maybe that was the place to start.

She moved closer to her father. "Dad, there's something I want to tell you."

He waited.

Her hand curled around something in her pocket. She smiled, recognizing the feel of Diggon's carving. "Sorry it's not a crane," he had said. "Beth tried to teach me, but I couldn't get all those folds."

She turned to her father. As her feelings began to unfold, she stroked the carving with her fingers. Rough wood sanded to a smooth satin finish. A Great Blue Heron, ready to fly.